A SEARCH FOR JUSTICE

Four Seasons Book 2

Jerry Schellhammer

PROMINENT
B O O K S
—— EDGE ——
5830 E 2nd St, Ste 7000 #9983
Casper, WY 82609
USA

ROADTRIP

2014

Mark focused on the here and now of October 15, 2014, drove down U.S. 2 heading towards Missoula in a Dodge Challenger Hector bought for him. *None of us have any idea what we're getting ourselves into here*, Mark said to himself as he looked at his old partner, Hector.

Mark then remembered a similar trip he and Hector took to become FBI agents back in 1990. He especially remembered an incident that made him appreciate Hector even more and thanking himself for not listening to his mother when he decided to take his .357 magnum Smith & Wesson. This road trip, for lack of a better word defined Mark as the man he had become, more than any other incident in his short life thus far.

"Hey Hector, remember that road trip we took across America back in 90?"

"Yeah, I remember," Hector, replied with a yawn.

"Did you have something to tell me?"

Hector turned to Mark with a blank expression on his fat face as he replied, "No Mark I don't."

"You don't have something you want to get off your chest?"

Hector shook his head, and said, "No I don't Mark; why are you asking?"

"No reason, just curious. Go ahead and take a nap. We still have an hour before Missoula."

February 1990

Che Lopez felt betrayed by his Federales when he received word of the agents' demise by Mark Marteau and Hector Gonzalez, a new player in this game he chose to be a part of. They both must go, he reasoned as he read the intelligence report from his contact, a Serbian named Osmet Vuk. Dressed conservatively, yet tastefully in gray suits and thin gray ties, he kept himself in the shadows with his pencil thin mustache under a long, thin nose and slick-back black hair and piercing brown eyes, to quietly observe whomever Che wanted watched.

Osmet arrived at Che's estate on this early winter's day of 1990 to discuss options with his employer about ridding him of Mark Marteau and Hector Gonzalez. Che stood in the shadows of his office as Osmet had difficulty adjusting his eyes to the purposefully dimmed light that filtered in from drawn venetian blinds. "Senor Lopez, it is good to see you," Osmet said.

"I'm sorry for the drawn blinds, but my skin condition, called photosensitivity, prevents me from having any sunlight on me. I break out so badly. I'm tempted to move to Canada in the winter, except I hate cold and snow," he replied chuckling at his attempt at humor.

"Yes, that would be quite the sacrifice to make," Osmet said as he located a nearby chair and sat upon it crossing his leg over his lap and watching the dark figure in front of him. Osmet tried to make out his face but only caught glimpses of what he thought were acne-like bumps teenaged boys possessed but appeared more pronounced.

"I want you to find out what this Mark Marteau and Hector Gonzalez are up to, and I want them eliminated. When you have found them, which I'm certain, given the intelligence you've given me so far you will have every opportunity at your disposal to quickly and efficiently take care of those two."

"I don't have to remind you that my price for this assignment will go up substantially," Osmet said quietly in his Serbian accented Spanish.

"I anticipated that would be the case. I arranged that you would receive a substantial increase in your monthly salary, say twenty thousand American more. Would that be satisfactory for you?"

"Very much so," Osmet replied with a thinnest of smiles to compliment his mustache. He immediately stood up and said, "I will give you updates." He left Che's office, went outside into the heat of the February afternoon, climbed inside his recently purchased BMW 3i, and drove away from the compound.

March 1990

March 4, 1990 held little in the affairs of the world that defined Mark's life, except for two things. Mark bought himself a 1980 Dodge Aspen station wagon that he tried to place a positive spin upon, though he knew, it had nothing on his 'Cuda. This car, Mark knew needed serious work to make it road worthy. The engine needed a complete tune-up, as well as replacement for a master cylinder, a cracked windshield and four bald tires.

"Why did you buy this thing," his dad, Jack asked him when he drove home, as exhaust smoke turned away any mosquitos hovering about the neighborhood trying to get an easy meal.

Mark moved back with his parents to recover from his injuries following the nasty shootout in Baja California. Hector continued to work for the American Consulate in Tijuana, but letters he recently received from Hector indicated his time there appeared to be drawing to a closed and he was looking for work somewhere else.

Mark looked at his father with a hurt expression on his face but explained evenly, "Dad, it's a Dodge; we're Mo-Par people, and it will give me something to do while I'm recovering."

For all intents and purposes Jack Marteau was a twenty-two-year older version of his son. Though his a large beer belly had replaced the six-pack abs he had back in his day, his brown hair had started to darken and gray, and his chin had doubled, hung loosely in front of his large neck, he still held himself with high regard and continued to be an intimidating presence to Mark.

"Son, this car is a piece of shit, and I'm sure you know it. You have all that money in your savings; why don't you at least buy a slightly used car? Those K-cars are nice and reliable. And, I hear those Dodge Magnums are nice to look at too."

"I can make it work, Dad. Trust me; I know what I'm doing."

"I sometimes wonder if you really do, son," Jack replied doubtfully as he went back inside the house. "That car better not be leaking oil on my driveway either," he called out before he closed the door.

Mark kept his post office box open from his bounty hunting business days and would often stop by the post office to see if he received mail. On this day, he received a letter from Hector and Mark opened it immediately.

> "Hey there Bro,
>   I got this thing in the mail looking for FBI agents. I'm gonna apply and I think you should too.
>
>   See you around,
>   Hector"

Mark read it again and then took the letter home, so he could think on it. He hadn't lost that much in strength as he could attest by working on his Aspen Wagon. On occasion, he would go to the police academy shooting range just north of town on Horn Road and shoot some paper targets from twenty-five feet using his .357 magnum; just to keep an edge, should someone try to break into his parents' house.

I should do this, Mark reasoned. *I can't keep doing what I'm doing now—living at Mom and Dad's and not contributing to the greater good.* He finished replacing spark plugs, went inside, and made some phone calls before he connected to the right person, none other than Chief of Police Tracie Dickerson.

"I've been waiting for you to call, Mark. What the heck is going on?"

"Well, I received this letter from Hector Gonzalez today and he's going to enlist in the FBI. I'm thinking about doing that too."

"Hell, if you want my blessing, then you got it. You'd make a fine FBI agent, son."

"Well, thanks, but I need to know what the process is. Where do I go and who do I see?"

"Well, I would suggest you march your butt down to the Federal Building there in Richland and apply. If they don't have the information, then someone there would or should know someone else who can help you, Mark."

"Thanks, Tracie. I'll go down there and apply," Mark replied as he wrote down, "federal building and get number," on a note pad next to the wall mounted avocado green phone that had been a part of the Marteau household for over twenty years. "How are you doing, Chief?"

"I'm running for Benton County Sheriff," the chief boasted proudly.

"I thought you were above that political b.s."

"Hell, I'm pissed at the current sheriff and I think enough common folk, like yourself, are equally pissed off too; enough so I could beat him in November."

"Good luck with that," Mark said sardonically. "I'll vote for you, though."

"Well, good luck to you, Mark. I'll talk with you later. Bye."

The next day Mark went to the Federal Building and the security guard, sitting behind a metal desk with imitation wood grain top, who could have passed as a Jimmy Durante impersonator, directed him to the Human Resources Office, where Mark greeted a much younger looking and attractive woman with her hair wrapped in a bun upon her head. "Hello there, I'm Mark Marteau and I would like an application for the FBI."

"Well, I'd be more than happy to help you," she replied upon seeing this big young man dressed in a double-breasted suit that appeared to have been bought at an estate sale. Mark held his wide brimmed Fedora in his hand as he looked favorably towards her too.

She went to the back, opened a file drawer from a tall file cabinet, and pulled out a book, in Mark's eyes, sealed inside a manila envelope as she walked back to Mark and handed him the massive package. "I'm sorry if this looks intimidating, but we are talking about the federal government, and they want to know everything. I do mean everything, and there will be a thorough background check done as well; so, don't try to hide anything either, it will only get you into trouble."

"I knew there was a reason I never liked the government," Mark reasoned. "Well, right now I have nothing but time on my hands. I'll fill this monstrosity out and…who do I turn this in to?"

"Inside there is an address you will need to send the package to; it's in Washington, D.C.," Cindi replied as Mark noticed the name on the picture I.D. badge clipped upon her blouse above the vie of her neckline. Mark suddenly remembered her from 1977 when she served him and Dave at that Denny's restaurant prior to that fateful meeting the night that his life changed forever. He chose not to remind her, though. Sometimes, he reasoned, it's best to keep the past in the past.

He hated filling out applications and this really made him angry because they wanted to know every detail from his past. "It's like they want to invade my privacy, but I'm doing it willingly just, so I can get this job," he bitterly said to himself aloud as his mother busied herself in the kitchen cooking dinner. In front of him were opened phone directories for all the businesses he has ever worked for, as well as all his personal and professional associates he ever had dealings with, who could be useful in him getting this job. He purposefully left Nicole out, though. She would ruin everything, he reasoned. *She knows too much from my bad old days and that would hurt my chances more.*

Well after midnight, he signed the last page of this book, as Mark called it, and placed it in a manila envelope, which he planned to mail the next day when the post office opened. He copied down the mailing address onto the front and placed the package inside, sealing it tightly. *I will pay for metered postage tomorrow, rather than use up all my stamps.* His parents had long since gone to bed as he sat in the living room on the couch that sat in front of the fireplace. On top of the mantle held his high school graduation picture that his mother seemed to cherish above all else.

Mark had tried to go back to smoking, but he coughed unmercifully and ended up grinding out the cigarette, cursing himself that he wasted three dollars for two packs of cigarettes he could not smoke anymore. The surgeon at the Tijuana hospital, who removed the destroyed lung, told him not to smoke.

"Your one remaining lung wouldn't handle it," he warned.

He threw the twin packs of Camel 99s in the trash can and walked away. "I should have done this two years ago," He exclaimed.

Every day he went into downtown Richland, he would stop by an auto parts store and pick up something that needed replacement. *The car is old enough, I don't have to hire some mechanic to do the work for me. Not like today's cars that have all that extra crap on the engine and computers that break down after a couple years and you must pay a fortune to get fixed or the car won't run anymore.*

It took eight weeks before he received a letter from the Federal Bureau of Investigation wanting him to report to the Spokane Federal Building to go through a physical and an initial interview. Mark had just finished buying four new radial tires for his Aspen and decided to take it to Spokane to see how she handled. The 223-cubic inch inline six wasn't much for power, but it had good fuel economy.

It took him two and a half hours to drive there at the posted sixty miles per hour speed limit. Other cars passed him by as if he stood still. However, the car gave him no concerns as it cruised along nicely on the four-lane freeway. After he passed the airport exit, he saw the high rises of the Spokane skyline and felt a sense of relief that he made it here without incident.

Mark initially had a hard time figuring out the one-way streets of this town and became increasingly frustrated by the entire situation, until he finally found the Spokane Federal Building and parked in the rear parking area that required he pay two dollars to park. "Two dollars," he yelled at the ticket validator machine. He inserted the two rolled up dollar bills and watched the ticket pop out.

When the doctors had finished with him and he had dressed back into his burgundy double-breasted suit he bought at Good Will especially for this day, he saw the man who would interview him. Mark saw right away the badge on his dark gray suit read Joseph Armstrong. He arose from his chair across from a steel desk from a bygone era and extended his hand to Mark, who shook it quickly but firmly. "Mark Marteau," Mark said to the man with short blonde hair and clean-shaven face. He looked to be in his mid to late thirties with slender build and Mark sensed he worked out regularly.

"Joe Armstrong," Joe replied as he returned the same hand pressure and offered Mark the chair in front of him. "I must say Mr. Marteau; I'm pleasantly surprised by your experience in law enforcement. You started as an informant and then became a bounty hunter...I see also, you worked security for a year at Hanford, but you were terminated. I cannot fault you for that one, security is very boring, and I would not wish it on anyone our ages, or younger. You took criminal justice at Washington State University. I don't see that you graduated though."

"I had a hard time concentrating on the subjects. I passed the tests okay, but the reading stuff—I don't know—it bored the heck out of me. I'm more of hands on kind of person. All that book learning stuff, the theories and all that, didn't do a thing for me and just didn't continue in my final year."

"I see. You do realize that the FBI requires a minimum BA or BS degree, preferably masters? Would you have objections to continuing your education after completing initial FBI training?"

"Personally, I'd rather not, but, if it is something that would benefit me professionally, then I will definitely do that."

"I admire your honesty Mr. Marteau. Both Georgetown University and VCU offer criminal justice degree programs and I'm fairly certain your earned credits are transferable."

"Okay, then when do I start?"

"When you have passed the physical and psychological evaluations, I will contact you and set up another interview, probably within a week. Finally, after you clear the initial background check, you'll be given your orders to go to FBI Training academy at Quantico, Virginia."

"That sounds good enough for me. Tell me, a friend of mine, Hector Gonzalez is going through the process too. Do you know how far along he is?"

"Even if I did, and I don't; I couldn't tell you anyway; that's highly confidential information, Mr. Marteau."

Mark stood up and reached his hand over to Special Agent Armstrong, who also arose from his desk and firmly shook his hand as he said to him, "I'll let you know within a week, Mr. Marteau."

On the way back home while Mark concentrated on the long drive ahead of him, he noticed a black BMW coming up on him like he stood still and passed him, seemingly moving over into Mark's lane as he did, causing Mark to veer sharply right to avoid hitting the car. "You stupid son of a bitch," Mark yelled at the offending driver as he continued down the freeway. Mark seriously thought about going after the person except for one important issue; Mark couldn't be certain if the Dodge Aspen could keep up with the newer car. He did his best to calm his nerves as he slowly breathed in and out through his nose, as both Dave and Hector taught him whenever some idiot enraged him.

He made it home without incident. *But, I had better be on the lookout for that asshole in the future.* When he glimpsed at the driver, he saw him to be a white guy with black hair and a thin mustache. *I wish I got his license plate number. I'll keep this under my hat, though.*

A month later, Mark received his orders to go to Quantico and received a call from Hector. "Hector is that really you?"

"Yeah, it's me, man. What's going on up there in Washington?"

"I just received my marching orders to go to Quantico, How about you?"

"Yeah, I'm going in two weeks."

"We should go there together."

"Oh, I don't know man. We would have to meet somewhere. It sounds more like a hassle than anything else."

"Hector, just come up here then."

"Unlike what you may have been told, amigo, not all Mexicans willingly go up there. It's fucking cold up there, man."

"I think you're messing with me," Mark replied sardonically.

"Yeah, I am dude."

Mark heard a knocking on the door just then. "Someone's at the door. Hang on a moment."

"Hey, call me back, bye." He disconnected the call.

"Dammit Hector; I'm just going to answer the door." Mark placed the house phone back on the hook of the wall mounted antique from a bygone era that his father refused to give up.

Hector caught Mark totally off guard when he answered the door. *How the hell does he know where my parents live?*

"Hey Bro, you look like I caught you with your pants down playing hide the bone with Miss Sally Tight-Twat."

"Hector, come on in. How the hell did you know where I lived at?"

"That was easy, Mark," Hector replied with his familiar toothy grin. "I just went to the County Assessor over there in Kennewick and they were more than happy to provide me that information."

"I guess there really is no privacy when your own government gives away peoples' addresses," Mark said with a bitter edge to his voice.

"Oh no, man; I had to pay them assholes to give me your address."

"Money does open doors," Mark said with more bitterness in his voice when he closed the door and led Hector into the living room. "Why didn't you just call to let me know you were coming?"

"What, and miss seeing you with that expression on your face as you opened the door; that was priceless." Hector laughed at his friend's expense.

"Well, now that you caught me, as you said, with my pants down, I guess we can make our plans."

It became Hector's turn to look like a deer in headlights as his eyes got really big, "What plans?"

"Plans to do this road trip, you dufus," Mark replied to his friend.

"I just thought we were going to fly over there."

"Why fly when we have a perfectly good running car that will get us there ten times cheaper. I want to drive and see this great and wonderful country. God knows we'll be flying until the cows come home for the length of our careers. I want to be like that Jack Kerouac guy that went cross country in a micro bus back in the sixties."

"This is kind of sudden, Mark. Are you sure we can get there in time? What are you going to drive in? No, you aren't even suggesting driving that wagon sitting in the driveway, leaking oil all of three thousand miles."

"Well yeah. And it ain't leaking no oil."

"Okay, that black splotch on the driveway isn't oil; sure, now tell me what the hell is it then?"

"It's probably dirt or something," Mark replied getting increasingly more frustrated by his friend's reluctance to do this.

"I want to test drive that car before I agree to do this, Mark."

"That's fine, I have no problem with that," he said defensively.

"Good, we'll start tomorrow," Hector said as he sat on the couch and looked at the picture of Mark sitting on the fireplace mantel. "Damn you were an ugly kid; hell man, you're still ugly. But at least you have good looking sisters."

"Hector, you can go and kiss my ass." Hector laughed and then Mark laughed too as they both got up and hugged each other. "I missed you man. I had hoped you would have made up here to see that trial of Lopez-Sanchez."

"How did that turn out?"

"The judge, upon my advice, reduced his sentence from fifty to life in the state pen, to twenty years at a federal super max somewhere in Colorado."

"That's really harsh dude. I know you wanted to see that son of a bitch fry for ordering that hit on your friend."

"Yeah, well he's in such a deep hole none of his associates can dig him out until 2008. He'll be too damn old to be of much use to anyone when he gets out of there."

"Yeah, you're probably right dude. Where are your parents at?"

"They went to a church pot-luck and will be home around seven. Just in time for Jeopardy, that's their favorite show," Mark said.

Hector looked at Mark a moment and then asked in all seriousness, "Is your dad like you?"

"What do you mean, Hector," Mark asked innocently.

"Oh, I think you know, Mark; Make stupid statements about Mexicans that come across as racist."

"Oh, he's nothing like me. He tolerates those people. The only reason I like you is because you act normal, not like them other Mexicans."

"Well, that's refreshing."

"My mom on the other hand, can't stand anyone that ain't white and Republican. I get her bent on things political."

"So, it's your mother that I need to worry about, then."

"Yeah, she thinks Reagan is a god and should be canonized when he dies," Mark stated proudly. "She also thinks the Ku Klux Klan is misunderstood."

"What the hell is there to misunderstand with them assholes? They hate all people that aren't white, Baptist and squeaky-clean conservative."

"Well, she believes you need people like that to appreciate good Republican values."

"Damn, Mark; your family is messed up."

"I'm glad you think so," Mark replied as he heard a car pull up in the driveway. "Oh, speak of the devil, here they are now."

They both stood up and waited for the front door to open. Jack walked in first as Hector saw a twenty plus year older version of Mark with salt and pepper hair and a good size beer gut that covered his midsection. He at first looked at Mark, then Hector, and back at Mark again nodding in Hector's direction, waiting for an introduction.

Mary came in next as she had a huge grin upon her face that suddenly disappeared the second she saw Hector standing in her living room. Hector got the impression of her bigotry the instant she saw him, and he felt the tension in the room heighten tenfold. "Hello, may I help you?" Mary asked in a frosty tone.

"Yeah, I'm Hector Gonzalez, Mark's guardian angel, who wouldn't be alive today if it weren't for me saving him twice."

"Oh, so you're the Mexican that Mark has high praises for," she replied as her smile returned, but Hector didn't trust it. "What brings you all the way up here? Picking season won't start up for another couple of months."

Why isn't Mark saying something to her? Hector thought as he glanced at Mark. "Mark and I are going to Washington, DC to train in the FBI academy," Hector replied choosing to ignore her underhanded comment. *Come on Mark talk to her.*

"I see," Mary replied. "Mark, you never told me you and he were going to the FBI. When did you decide to go this route?"

"About two months ago; Hector sent me a letter telling me about a recruiting being done and that I should apply too. I know I told you about it."

"Oh, of course you did," Mary replied still looking at Hector like an intruder rather than a guest in her home. "I totally forgot you mentioned it, son. Well, I'm sure you'll need to go back to your Motel 6 or Travel Lodge in East Pasco, or wherever your kind goes to. You can visit Mark somewhere tomorrow. Goodbye now, it's been nice to meet you."

"Mom, he's staying here with us tonight, and for the next three nights until we leave for Washington," Mark stated to her with the authority that there would be no further discussion about it.

"I see. I thought maybe he would prefer to be with his own kind, rather than here where he's obviously not welcomed," Mary replied staring down at Hector.

"You know what, Mark, she's right I would much rather go someplace where I would feel welcomed. What was the name of that place up by that mall?"

"Did you mean Cavanaugh's?" Mark asked knowing he had just added gasoline to the fire.

"Yeah, that's the place. My credit card has a ten-thousand-dollar limit should handle whatever the cost may be. You're invited to come too, Mark."

"I appreciate the offer, but I think I'll stay here tonight," Mark replied as he glanced at his mother, whose face showed crimson with rage as they walked outside together. "I think we both pissed her off really well," Mark said as they walked to Hector's rental, a 1989 Buick Regal.

"She definitely is proud of her opinions, I see," Hector said with an ironic edge. "I have to say, I never met a no holds barred racist before. She's right; you, or I, appreciate the Republican Party more because of people like her. I would have appreciated a little help from you in there, Mark. But, hey it's no big deal now. I can handle people like her; always have." He got behind the wheel of his rental car and said, "Call me when you're ready to go." He started the car and drove off.

"Well, Mom I hope that you're proud with yourself," Mark said as he walked into the house. "I would have expected this if he was some asshole Spic off the streets wanting a hand out, but, like Hector stated, he saved my bacon down there."

"It's of no importance now," she replied as she and Jack watched Jeopardy. Alex read a clue about a capital in the Balkans region where the Olympics were held. "What is Sarajevo?" Mary answered before one of the contestants rang in.

"Besides Mark, you shouldn't have invited him here. You know how your mother feels towards those people," Jack interjected.

"He caught me totally by surprise too. He just came to the door. I thought he was still down in Mexico."

"Well, it just goes to show you can't trust those people," Mary responded. "A white man wouldn't just come to someone's home unannounced like that."

The next morning, Mark sat in front of Cavanaugh's Hotel, a two story three or four-star affair where Mark would go on a Friday or Saturday night to listen to a local rock or blues band perform as he hunted for a one-night stand. He pulled out his cell phone and called Hector's cell, who answered with a raspy sounding voice, "Hello?"

"You're still in bed?" Mark asked his friend incredulously.

"Shit, man I'm sorry; I must've overslept. Give me ten minutes and I'll be right down." He disconnected the call and Mark folded his cell phone and placed it back inside his suit pocket of a gray double-breasted suit jacket, as he stepped back inside his Dodge Aspen. He fiddled with the newly installed stereo system with CD player and JVD speakers. He felt proud of himself, when it came to doing the repairs to this car; he had everything completed that needed repaired. It also helped that he had the money to make the necessary repairs.

It just did not look all that great as it still had dings and dents on the sides where other peoples' car doors had nailed her over the years, the windshield was still cracked, and the rubber door stripping had dry rotted so bad that Mark could hear the wind as he drove down the highway.

Hector finally came outside. Mark could tell by his scruffy look, his disheveled shaggy hair and the bags under his brown eyes, that Hector spent more time than was necessary in the hotel's lounge. He seemed to walk slowly toward the car as Mark observed him through rearview mirror.

He immediately went to the passenger seat and sat down. "This car smells like cigarette smoke," he complained right off the bat.

"Well, good morning to you too, sunshine," Mark replied. "I take it you did a little bender last night."

"Yeah, well having to be nice to your mother so neither you nor your dad would beat the crap out of me for telling her what I really thought of her, made me so mad that I couldn't stop thinking about it and drown myself in booze instead."

"She has a way about her," Mark replied singing out from a Billy Joel song.

"Hey, don't torture me with your lame attempt at singing."

"Sorry amigo; I see you're in no shape for driving, so I'll take the wheel and show you how this thing runs. I fixed it up good and got the major stuff that was wrong with it taken care of. The rest is pretty much cosmetic; I'm not going to concern myself with that," Mark said as he instinctively buckled his seat belt, started the car, placed it in reverse and pulled out from the parking lot.

"I drove it up to Spokane for the interview and it ran well. It gets good fuel mileage too."

"Hey, you don't need to sell me this bucket of bolts; I just want to see how it rides. You said you were going to take us on a road trip?

"Well, yeah a short jaunt to show you how she performs. I thought we could go to the Blue Mountains and back; out to Dayton and turn around and take a little detour through Walla Walla and head back here. It will be a nice day trip," Mark said as he moved the car through the heavy morning commute traffic. "Damn congestion in this town has gotten so bad lately," Mark complained as he took the exit onto renamed State Route 241.

"Probably has to do with all those beaners coming up here from California," Hector said bitterly.

"I'm sure that has something to do with it," Mark replied, not even thinking who he was talking to.

Hector laughed a laugh born from frustration and anger. "Shit man, your family is all fucked up. I hope, while we're doing this road trip of yours, you can keep your opinions under wraps, especially when we go through cities like Chicago."

"I'll try to heed your advice," Mark replied evenly.

"I know you're used to saying stuff that, to you, it may seem logical, but is really very ignorant. I won't be able to help you out of too many scrapes if you say something that will piss people off and make me look like a fool if I defended you."

"I'm sorry my parents didn't live up to your ideal of a great American family," Mark snapped back angrily.

"They were brought up in the past where that kind of mindset was tolerated, Mark. You on the other hand, should have flat told your parents they were wrong and live your life your way without being brainwashed by their ignorance," Hector replied. Mark knew he made sense, but felt so angry, he couldn't do anything more than react the only way he knew how.

"The white race is and always will be the superior race. Look at history and it will show you the truth," Mark rebutted.

"So, the hell what," Hector replied. "The white race can go fuck themselves for all I care; that's not what I'm trying to tell you. If you want to become a good FBI agent, you have got to learn tolerance and respect people of their skin color."

"Fine," he replied seething at Hector's logic. "I'll do it, but I won't like it."

"It won't much matter whether you like it or not; it's the decent thing to do, or you'll end up bitter and angry with the world, like your mother."

Mark sighed heavily as he crossed the Blue Bridge and ended up skirting around Pasco and heading south to a very small town called Burbank. "Can we change the subject, now?"

"Sure, we can change the subject. My, what a beautiful day we picked to take this little jaunt," Hector said as he seemingly saw the clear and sunny June morning for the first time. "That wind, though had a nasty bite to it."

"Yeah, but it will warm up soon enough," Mark replied as his anger started to ebb a bit. "This town here is Burbank. It ain't much, though; I'm not even sure how this town even came about or who it was named after. After a bit we'll be coming upon three smaller towns called Waitsburg, Prescott and Dayton. I like to refer to them as the mini-Tri-Cities, though I'm sure the people who live there don't see it that way."

"I'm sure they wouldn't either," Hector replied as he watched the open crop circles and the mechanical sprinklers pushing water onto immature crops, whose green leaves just begun to sprout up from the fertile brown loam. "How long is this road trip, anyway?"

"All told, it shouldn't be more than four hours," Mark replied as he crossed his fingers.

"Yeah, well you convinced me how road worthy this car is. Let's make our plans then," Hector said as he turned to face Mark. "Do you have a road map here?"

"Yeah, it's in the glove box," he replied. He glanced at Hector a second while the unofficial navigator fished the map out from the glovebox and unfolded it to reveal a predetermined route he already planned on taking long before he told Hector of this. On the map, he had penciled in the route he wanted to take, making circles on cities or towns where they would spend the night, approximately twelve hundred miles apart, staying mostly on the interstate from Tri Cities through Eastern Oregon and through Idaho, Wyoming, Nebraska, Missouri, Illinois, Kentucky, Pennsylvania and Virginia.

"Well, shit Bro you pretty much already got this thing planned out."

"Yeah, I figured with both of us driving three-hour shifts, we should be well rested and stuff. Then, we can stop at any Motel along the way after about twelve hours of driving."

"Hey, well what else do we need to do?" Hector asked Mark hoping everything else was in order.

"I want to buy us groceries, saving us money on food. I don't trust half those diners anyway. Remember about not drinking the water in Mexico? Well, it pretty much is the same in some of these diners in America. Plus, they charge more than if we just go and buy food from a grocery store," Mark rationalized.

"Okay, I have no problem with that; we should probably bring a cooler to store water or something.

No alcohol though," Hector said as he raised his hand swearing off the stuff.

"You have no argument from me, Hector. I've been low key when it comes to drinking. I did have a problem coming home from Spokane and want to bring my .357 along too."

"I also brought my gun; you'd like it, it's a Colt .45 I bought at the Army Surplus Store. What kind of problem did you have?"

"It might have been nothing, but on the way back some asshole in a black BMW nearly ran me off the road. A feeling came over me that it might not be the last time our paths cross and I want to be ready for him."

"That might be serious," Hector agreed. "You do have a couple enemies still living in Mexico that would like nothing better than to see you dead."

"Yeah, well I ain't worried. Besides, they'll have to do more than try and run me off the road to get my attention," Mark replied boastfully, though inwardly he wondered who else would be going after him.

Hector gave his friend sidelong glances as he slowly shook his head. "Do you know someone by the name Che Lopez?"

"Not really, am I supposed to?"

"Um, he runs the Lopez Cartel down in Baja California and word has it, he might be, or already has, put a hit on you," Hector replied. "I'd be especially careful, amigo."

"Your warning is well taken," Mark said as they began driving into a more wooded area and the town of Waitsburg came into view. "This is a pretty sad little town. I don't even know what keeps it going."

"I would bet there are a lot more to this town than you would give it credit for," Hector replied. "If you see woods, then there must be game and there must be plenty of hunters that come here to hunt that game. They most likely spend money on things like food and ammo and whatever else one needs to be successful."

"Yeah, I suppose you're right," Mark replied.

"I've seen enough, let's go back and get you packed and ready to go," Hector said.

Osmet kept a low profile as he went about gathering intelligence on this man, Mark Marteau. The only thing he found interesting about him was his inclination to purchase old suits from the 30s and 40s. *Why does he spend money on something from a bygone era?* He asked himself.

He decided to follow him up to Spokane to determine what this special trip appeared to be. He nonchalantly followed Mark inside the Federal Building, pretending to be lost as he noticed him going into an elevator that stopped at the fifth floor.

"Excuse me, I seemed to be a bit lost; what building is this?" he asked the receptionist who smiled broadly at his foreign accent,

"You are at the Federal building," she told the man very slowly and loudly, uncertain how much English he knew. "May I help you find something?"

"What is on the fifth floor?"

"That is where the FBI has their offices," she smiled evenly, uncertain how much information might be too much for this man with the Eastern European accent. "Do you need to speak with someone in the FBI?"

"No, I thought I recognized an old friend going up there earlier," Osmet replied. "I am sorry to have bothered you. Have a nice day, young lady." He walked away and went outside where he pulled his cell phone from his gray jacket pocket. He called Che directly to his private line. "It appears he has joined the FBI," he told him in Serbian.

"That is interesting. You will have to eliminate him before he goes to report for their training academy. I wonder if his Mexican friend has done the same thing?"

"I did intercept a letter two months ago from Hector. It could be a safe bet they have both joined this organization."

"If that is the case, we should probably see how they plan to travel to this FBI academy. Where is this academy, anyway?"

"I believe it is at a place in Virginia called Quantico," Osmet replied as he caught a couple people giving him hard glances as he talked Serbian to the cell phone.

"We can hope they decide to fly there, so we can have them both eliminated at the airport."

"That would be the best possible scenario," Osmet agreed. "I will confirm when I find out what they plan to do."

"Very well, Osmet, I will hear from you when you have more information." Osmet heard the line disconnect. He placed his phone back inside his jacket pocket and waited inside the parking garage near Mark's dinged-up car, an American brand called Dodge Aspen.

Mark appeared preoccupied and didn't even glance at Osmet, when he got inside and turned the ignition. He watched Mark pull out and drive from the garage and into the city traffic, slowly making his way out of Spokane. Osmet followed from a discreet distance.

After they had made their way upon the freeway and eventually became the only two vehicles on the divided highway, Osmet decided to test this Mark's character a bit. He shifted his BMW 3i into third, noting the RPMs jumping up noticeably as it gained speed and he came quickly upon Mark, who apparently never paid Osmet any heed while he passed him.

Osmet then quickly jerked his steering wheel towards the ugly American car, forcing Mark to veer sharply to the right to avoid getting hit as Osmet drove on as if nothing had happened. He waited to see if this man would become enraged enough to try and confront him, but he never did, which made Osmet slightly disappointed. *There will be another time my friend,* Osmet said to himself.

Mark and Hector planned to leave in two days as they did the necessary preparations. Mark purposefully stayed clear of his mother, not wanting a confrontation where Hector was concerned. Mark loved his mother and knew her beliefs became his beliefs and it never occurred to him that those beliefs, as Hector stated, were born out of ignorance and fear, rather than something nostalgic, from a time long ago where such views were accepted.

They went to the police academy outside Richland and did target practice with their respective handguns the next day, just to give them both an edge of confidence. Mark came home afterwards.

After cleaning the pistol, Mark packed his handgun inside an overnight bag he planned to take along, sitting beside him all the way to Virginia. Mary walked into the room he had lived in these past twelve months, and for six years before that.

"Why are you avoiding me?" she asked in a demanding manner.

"I've been busy, that's all," Mark replied evasively.

"Does it have to do with that Mexican friend of yours?"

"Yes, Mom it has to do with that Mexican friend of mine."

"I don't know why you chose him to be your friend, of all people. They can't be trusted, Mark. Their entire strategy is to take over this country, like the Russians tried to do until Reagan came into office and he bankrupted that evil empire."

"Hector isn't anything like that Mom. He's actually a decent man, and he saved my ass down there, twice."

"I'm sure his brown heart is in the right place, but he's not one of us and he can't ever be one of us."

"You can't use a broad-brush stroke against every person and say they are alike. Hector went out of his way to become an American citizen, even joining the Marine Corps for four years."

"Maybe you're right, but it doesn't ever change how I feel about those people. How come you're bringing that gun with you?"

"It's called self-protection and it's called my God given right to bear arms granted to me by the second amendment."

"I wish you wouldn't; that could only invite trouble."

"I think it would be alright, Mom. Hector's bringing his too so that we'll have a way of defending ourselves should something go down."

"I love you, son but I'm not comfortable about you going on this trip, in that car, with that man, and taking a gun too, no less."

"I love you too Mom, but my mind is made up. The car is quite road worthy, Hector and I have been through a lot together, and undoubtedly, will continue well into the future of our careers in the FBI, and I am not leaving my gun here. It's coming with me." They hugged each other, and they kissed each other's cheeks.

"You have a safe trip," Mary told him before she reluctantly released her only son. "I have one more favor to ask you, my only son."

"I need to get packed, Mom. What is it?"

"I don't know how much longer Jack is going to be here. My biggest fear is losing my independence and having to live out my days in a nursing home filled with those people who I don't like or trust. Mark, please don't let me die alone."

"You and Dad are going to be fine. Yeah, sure I'll promise. We all end up dying some day; alone or with people you love." He kissed her cheek again— the one with the single tear falling without shame. "I plan to be safe too," Mark replied as he released from her.

Osmet camped outside the Marteau home that night and awoke when he heard the unmistakable Dodge high-pitched squeal of the starter engaging and the engine starting up. As he saw the big man sit inside the car and turned on the headlights, temporarily blinding him until Osmet turned his head. He saw the man drive pass him, drive down the street to Jadwin, and take a right, heading south.

Earlier, Osmet rifled through his potential victim's glove box. He saw the road atlas that this man planned to use to drive across this country to his destination. He noticed the first town that he circled with a black marker was North Platte, Nebraska. He located the key on the map and calculated the distance at around two thousand kilometers away. Osmet went about his plan and headed directly to North Platte, Nebraska where he would prepare a very rude end to those two men that Che Lopez wanted taken out. He did not mind driving these long distances. When he did holiday in Yugoslavia, he took his family to the high mountainous regions outside Transylvania. It was an area ripe with both history and fantasy that he loved to explore and research. Unfortunately, his wife and two children never shared the same passion of history that he had.

He fueled his BMW 3i and began driving well ahead of his intended target. *I think,* Osmet said to himself as he massaged his pencil thin mustache, *I will find a couple of local boys to do the deed for me. I am certain they will find the presence of a brown-skinned man in their town a serious threat.* It did not appear to concern Osmet that a foreign man with an Eastern European accent, could also be construed as a threat to these local boys he intended to hire. He assumed the sight of a brown-skinned man would be more threatening to their shared bigotry than the speech patterns or accent of a foreign white man.

Mark and Hector would not know what scenario awaited them as Mark stopped in front of Cavanaugh's where Hector waited outside the lobby for him. "What took you so long, Bro," Hector asked slightly frustrated at his friend's tardiness.

"I overslept," Mark, replied apologetically.

"Well, unless you don't plan on stopping along the way to refuel ours and the car's tank, which I know we will, I don't foresee us getting to North Platt before 8 or 9 tonight. The sun is just now rising, and we haven't even left this town yet."

"I'm quite aware of that Hector. We'll have to add a couple miles per hour when it's advantageous," Mark replied as he maneuvered the Dodge wagon out from in front of the lobby area and onto Columbia Center Boulevard at 4:30 in the morning. Obviously, traffic was scarce at this time and Mark knew this, but also wanted to have started an hour ago as they had planned last night when they shopped at Costco just up the street from Cavanaugh's Hotel. That way, they calculated, they would miss the congestion of morning traffic in Boise and midafternoon traffic in Salt Lake City. Now, it would be more of a crapshoot as to how heavy the traffic would be in the next six to ten hours.

They drove east on State Route 241 and headed to the US 395 exit. They traveled south until they went to the I-84 exit just pass Hermiston, Oregon and headed east towards Pendleton. The freeway eventually meandered southerly, turned easterly again as the freeway crossed the Snake River and into Idaho. Hector proceeded to fall back to sleep before they left Kennewick. Mark drove through the twilight of early morning.

When the full light of morning shone brightest, they were heading due east into Idaho and Mark had to place his sunglasses over his eyes to protect him from the light, and in turn woke up Hector, who yawned loudly and stretched his arms. "Damn that felt good. You want me to take over and let you catch up on some zzzs?"

"Yeah, I probably should. The next gas station I come to, we'll top off the gas tank and you can take over."

"That works for me, amigo." They traveled twelve miles further when they reached a truck stop outside Napa. They both got out stretching, and Mark began fueling the gas tank while Hector went inside to pay for gas. Mark hadn't noticed that Hector had dressed in the same type of clothes he wore when they took their trip to Todos Santos in Baja California two years before.

Whatever made him comfortable, Mark reasoned to himself as he finished pumping gas. For his part

Mark opted to wear jeans and t-shirt with canvas sneakers, keeping his retro suits inside a garment bag. He went inside the car's passenger side, and waited for Hector to come out to take over driving. Hector had with him two syro-foam cups, stepped inside the car, and closed the door.

"I got you a hot cocoa and me a coffee."

"Thanks Hector, I appreciate it," Mark said as he took the hot cup from Hector's hand and set it on the plastic beverage holder that he mounted on the passenger door where the window frame began. "I'm gonna play a CD and jam out a bit until I fall asleep."

"Hey, no skin off my back, dude. So long as it ain't that gangster rap shit those kids are playing all the time now."

"I think you would know me better than that by now. I don't play anything but good old rock from the sixties and seventies." Mark went into the glove box to pull out a Led Zeppelin CD when he noticed something odd. "Someone's been in here going through my shit."

"How can you tell?" Hector asked trying to poke fun at his friend.

"No, seriously dude, some asshole went in and moved my shit around. Nothing's missing, but it wasn't how I set it up last night, neither."

"Was it your mom or dad?"

"I don't think so. Shit man, this has gotten me a little freaked out here," Mark said. Concern showed on his face as he finally found his CD and the road map that was folded very neatly, which was his first clue that someone had been rifling through his glove box. Mark purposefully folded the map, so his first destination would be visible. "This map is folded back to when I bought it at the mini-mart in Richland some three weeks ago."

"Well, like I said, amigo, your parents must have gone through for some reason. Who else could it have been?"

"I don't know." Mark suddenly felt a chill move quickly down his spine. I hope we brought enough firepower, Mark said to himself as he unbuckled his seat belt, turned himself around and pulled his first travel bag up and unzipped the first pocket, exposing his Smith & Wesson .357 magnum. He pulled the holstered weapon from the bag and kept it in front of him and then he buckled himself back in as Hector continued driving east on the interstate.

Hector, for his part didn't say a thing as the same chill ran down his spine too. I wish I had some friends in North Platt, he said to himself as he took more measures of traffic behind him as well as in front. He listened to the rocking beat from Jimmy Page and John Bonham when they started a classic tune that even Hector enjoyed listening to and heard Robert Plant belt out the first lyrics from the song "Kashmir," as he drove closer to their eventual destination.

Osmet arrived in North Platt around 7PM, though it seemed more like middle day to the Serb, who wasn't used to being this far north. He took the first exit and crossed onto the overpass, waiting for the American Dodge station wagon that he felt certain was an hour back. He listened to a very angry sounding man, named Rush Limbaugh, who preached to him a most passionate call for a conservative uprising against the current Bush Administration, a person he called weak and ineffectual.

He smiled at this angry American's voice. *What a foolish man. There is more to this world than what he has to offer. Yes, your President may be weak, but it is your people who elected him. He holds nothing to Marshall Tito, and never will. Marshall Tito has kept Yugoslavia together, by hook and crook since he defeated the Germans and told Stalin to back off; that he would be no puppet of the Warsaw Pact. I don't know what will happen when he is gone. There are already rumblings from Croatians and Bosnians wishing to be independent.*

He suddenly stopped his musings when he spotted the Aspen Wagon approaching and pulled up his binoculars to check the license plate. *Just as I suspect, yes, the same letters and numerals that I wrote on the license plate in that town called Richland.* He waited while the car went off the same exit that he took and watched the driver, who appeared to be the Mexican called Hector Gonzalez, taking a right turn and head toward the Motel 6 just up the four-lane street from the exit. Osmet quickly did an illegal U-turn, followed the wagon to the motel, and parked in the parking lot reserved for employees. He patiently waited for both men to appear from the motel's office and get back inside their car. He saw them drive twenty meters to a parking stall in front of room 19. He watched as they pulled out a pair of overnight bags from their car, went inside the room, and closed the door.

An hour later, they appeared in different clothes—Mark in his retro suit with large brim fedora and Hector slacks and western button-down shirt with cowboy boots and Stetson hat. Osmet assumed they refreshed themselves for a night on the town. This time, he saw Mark get inside behind the wheel while Hector rode shotgun.

They pulled from the motel and headed toward the town center and Osmet followed from a safe distance until they turned off at a low-key restaurant, many Americans call a "greasy spoon," called the Straw Hat Saloon. Osmet noticed the sky darken a bit, but assumed it was one of those lightning showers, which he remembered back in Yugoslavia. *I will wait for some low life scum to appear, who considers any man of brown skin pigment a threat.*

Twenty minutes later, such a group appeared coming in an older Ford pickup truck that smoked oil from its engine as it squeaked to a stop and a crew of four heavy set twenty to forty-year-old men jumped from the back. The equally large driver and passenger stepped down from the cab, sharing a filtered cigarette. *Perfect*, Osmet said to himself. *Six against two should be no match at all.*

Osmet also pulled himself out from his small BMW and walked up to the crew as he pulled out a Camel straight from a recently purchased pack and asked the bunch, "Gentlemen, please, do you have a match or light? I forgot when I bought these," he said in his heavily accented Serbian dialect.

The men stopped in their tracks as one. A burly man wearing a John Deere baseball cap started giggling at Osmet's accent. "Looky here boys, we got us a Russian come visit us. What the hell do you want, Ruskie?"

"I wish to have a light, please," Osmet replied evenly with a slight smile on his face. Another member of this crew pulled out a reusable plastic lighter and held it out for him as he flicked it twice before it flamed and Osmet graciously pulled on the cigarette, inhaling deeply as he exhaled a thick plume of smoke from his mouth. "Thank you very much. I have another favor to ask you gentlemen."

"Yeah, well we're all out of favors, Ruskie, the big man said with his typical mid-western dialect, that to Osmet's ear sounded no different than the southern dialect. "I suggest you get out of our way because we got us some serious beer drinking to do tonight."

Osmet watched them pass him and head toward the saloon's glass door when he said, "There's a Mexican in there that needs to be taught a lesson and I will pay you five thousand dollars to beat him to death."

"A Mexican?" The same big man stopped in his tracks and turned around as he saw the foreign man and asked, "What kind of beef do you have with this Mexican?"

"None, but I'm sure you, as a God-fearing American patriots, such as yourselves, must have many reasons," Osmet replied as he inhaled on his cigarette.

"Well, yeah we all do. Those fuckers steal our jobs and come in here illegally." Another member of the crew, a shorter wiry man, spit tobacco juice on the pavement to emphasize his disgust for the race.

"I'm sure you could all use five thousand dollars. It is after all a Friday night."

"Hell yeah, we could," the burly man replied. "Give us the money and we'll wipe that greaser's ass all over Jeffers Street."

"I'll give you the money after you do that ass wiping," Osmet replied.

"Ain't no skin off my teeth," the big man held his hand out for Osmet to shake, which he did as he recoiled from the big man's serious body odor. "Let's kick us some Mexican ass boys."

They piled inside the saloon whooping and hollering, and then all was quiet; eerily quiet when sirens began to wail and everyone inside piled out and headed around back. Osmet didn't understand what this situation that suddenly occurred was.

He saw the big man and yelled above the din of the wailing sirens, "What is happening?"

"There's a tornado coming this way you idiot. Turn around!"

Osmet did, as he never heard the term, "tornado" before. "What is tornado? Oh, shit," he screamed as he saw a funnel shaped cloud descend from the storm where lightning flashed angrily from the sky, reminding Osmet of the furies of hell reaping vengeance upon all mortals.

He ran quickly to his car and drove east on Phillips Street until he reached the Dead-End sign and a barricade of dirt and cinderblock just as he saw the funnel cloud following close behind. Just as suddenly, the tornado inexplicably disappeared, and the sirens ceased wailing.

Osmet went back to the Straw Hat Saloon and found nothing but an empty lot where only the interior portion of the building remained. The Dodge wagon had disappeared too. What happened to them? Osmet assumed they had gone with everyone else into the storm shelter, yet when everyone came up and out, surveying what remained of their beloved saloon, Mark and Hector were gone.

Hector saw the six men walk in before Mark did and realized something was not right the moment they walked in and began searching the dimly lit bar and pointed at him. "Mark, we might have a problem," Hector said nervously. Mark turned around to see what Hector was talking about when he saw the gang head towards them as one.

The tornado sirens went off and the middle-aged blonde bartender with a two-inch laceration scar on her right cheek announced, "Sorry boys, the bar is closed. Everyone head to the shelter."

Not a man in the bar argued with her but dutifully went out the front door where they filed toward the storm shelter located in the back. Mark spotted a black BMW speeding off heading east. *That looks like the same car that damn near ran me off the road,* Mark said to himself as he saw his first ever funnel cloud barreling down on the saloon and his Dodge in its direct path too.

"Let's get out of here," Mark told his friend as he bolted across the parking lot to his wagon and started it up.

"Are you crazy, man?" Hector followed quickly and went into the passenger seat as Mark slammed the shifter into drive and peeled out of there, barely missing a piece of shit looking Ford pickup.

Mark appeared to be driving directly at the incoming twister as Hector wondered if he too had lost his mind and prepared to bail from the car if it became apparent Mark planned to commit suicide. However, at the last possible second, Mark pulled to the left and veered away from the F2 twister. Hector turned around and saw the Straw Hat

Saloon explode into pieces and splinters. He saw a pipe fly through the rear window. He instinctively ducked. Shards of tempered glass flew into the back of the front seat, making a very audible bang sound that disintegrated the back window. "You are fucking crazy man," Hector yelled at his partner as they headed back to Motel 6.

"I think we have an unwelcomed guest," Mark told Hector as he pulled in front of Room 19 and got out of the car. "That BMW I told you about that tried to run me off the highway outside Spokane, I saw it speeding out of the parking lot before that tornado came down and destroyed that bar."

"Why did you take off like that, man?"

"I don't know about you, but I didn't feel like hanging around North Platte, Nebraska for how many days it would have taken to get a claim check from FEMA, or whoever handles that sort of thing and miss our orientation at Quantico."

"We could have bought another car, Mark. It's not like you didn't have no money to buy another. Were you worried about me?"

"I have no doubt that you could have handled yourself with a couple of those retards, but six would have been suicidal. I would have to kill three myself to even the odds and then we would still be stuck here trying to explain to the Lincoln County Sheriff about a possible hit from some guy driving a BMW."

"So, what do you want to do?"

Mark thought a moment. "Let's park the car somewhere, close enough so we don't have to hike all night, but away from here. So, if that guy shows up, he'll think we took off."

"I don't know; why don't we just take off and change our route entirely?"

"We could, I suppose, but you know what, Hector? I don't intend to away from that asshole. I don't shy away from a fight. If there is a hit on me, I want to face him man to man and see what he has."

"I hope, for your sake, we don't go after him; a hired assassin is no one to mess with amigo. He knows what he's doing; can you say the same thing about yourself?"

"I don't want to be looking over my shoulder the rest of my life, Hector, as I'm sure you don't either."

Hector shrugged his shoulders as he realized there was no arguing with Mark on this and privately prayed they wouldn't cross paths again with this mystery man driving a BMW. "I'll drive the car out back behind the motel," he said with a resigned sigh. "I'll be back in ten minutes."

Mark wasted no time as he moved the mattress from the bed and set it over the window. He kept the drapes drawn and did not turn on any of the lights. Darkness bathed the room as Hector stealthily came inside, closed and locked the door. "Help me move the other mattress over the door."

Hector helped Mark pull the mattress up against the door. "I'll stay up the first four hours and you can do the last four hours, then we'll take off," Hector told Mark. "I know it will be tough considering what we've been going through this pass hour or so, but at least try to get some shut eye."

"I take it, this isn't your first bike ride; shit what am I saying? Of course, it's not. You seem to be in your own element when it comes to this sort of thing," Mark said.

"Yeah, well I went to Grenada and did some drug interdiction in Colombia and Bolivia while I served in the Marines," Hector said. "I saw some shit and yeah, I think better and feel more within myself when I'm in this sort of situation. You didn't do too shabby yourself amigo, when we did that shit in Baja California and this afternoon too. I would have taken my chances with them assholes in that storm shelter, rather than take off like a bat out of hell like that."

"I react better when my life is on the line. The moment I spotted that BMW peeling away, I knew we had better chances beating that tornado than trying to beat those six redneck assholes in that storm shelter. It could have gotten ugly in there."

Hector nodded as the shadows of night made the room darker. "In case we get into a gun battle with that asshole, we need an exit strategy. You were smart to let me move that car. He may well think that we already left town and is heading to our next destination. But, if he thinks otherwise and wants to shoot our room out; it's a safe bet he followed us here earlier when we arrived. For shits and giggles, he might just decide to fire up this place and let God count the innocents."

"I checked the back window over the bathtub. It would be too tight for me, but you should make it out okay. My thought being is that you could outflank him and take him out while I'm firing a diversion."

"You been watching a lot of war movies, haven't you, amigo?"

"I watched my fair share, but there must be some truth to this crap, even for Hollywood."

"Yeah, you're right. That is how we do these things; try to do a flanking move where they aren't expecting and take them out." I suggest you lay down try to get some sleep, amigo. You got a long drive ahead of you first thing in the morning."

Mark moved over to a far corner of the room where the bed frame and headboard stood. Mark threw a bed sheet over him and soon began snoring fitfully. Hector looked at his watch; it read 9:14 on the analog dial. *I'll wake him at 1:30 and then I can snore like a freight train. When he wakes me, I'll drive and let him sleep for a few hours. Damn, this has gotten complicated. There was no way of knowing though.*

Out of curiosity, Hector quietly moved over to the mattress-covered window and peeked his head out just enough for him to see outside at an oblique angle so that he could only see the northeast portion of the parking lot. *No sign of him from this angle,* Hector sighed. He carefully pulled himself back and slowly, carefully made his way to the other side of the window and repeated the same process as before, and found everything, as much as he could see, appeared clear of this assassin.

Each hour that passed Hector repeated the same routine, ensuring this person in a black BMW wasn't there. *Maybe he did move on to the next location.* Hector remembered to grab the map from the glove box and went into the bathroom where he closed and locked the door. He pulled out his military issued periscope flashlight with the red filter and turned it on while he looked at the next destination on the map. He saw where Mark had penciled in Youngwood, Pennsylvania as the next place that seemed to junction two main interstates, taking I-72 south towards Virginia and eventually Quantico, and their destination that he circled in bright red marker. Hector checked his watch and he saw it was Mark's turn to do the watch. *I hope that all will be quiet*, Hector said to himself as he shook Mark awake. "It's your turn amigo."

Osmet lost them and now there would be hell to pay for this inexcusable error. He cursed himself bitterly. *Where could they have gone? I know eventually their destination will lead them to this FBI academy in Quantico, Virginia, but my job was to eliminate them long before that time. Could they be back at that motel?* He decided to drive by there. *After all*, he reasoned, *they would at least need to grab their belongings first.*

But, when he went back to the Motel 6 and saw the parking space empty and the room dark, he sighed and pounded his steering wheel out of frustration. It never occurred to Osmet that they had the wherewithal to hide out the night inside the motel room with their mattresses barricading the door and window. *They must have gone to their next destination.* He checked his notepad and saw it to be the town of Youngwood, Pennsylvania. *I will drive there and hope I can catch up to their car and hope I can take them out.* He noticed when he studied the map last night how this man had drawn out a precise plan where they would travel a certain distance in twelve hours, where they would rest for the night and spend the last eight hours getting to Quantico, Virginia.

He began driving east on Interstate 80 and drove as far as Ralston, Nebraska just outside Omaha, where his mind and body screamed at him to pull off and get some sleep. After 21 hours of driving close to 1521 miles, he could drive no further and found a motel that he checked-in. The man, who took his money and glanced at his ID, a forged West German drivers' license, looked at him with a high degree of suspicion.

"Where did you say you were from?" He asked with that same Midwestern drawl that made Osmet wince.

"I don't believe I did," He replied tersely, hoping he would get the hint that Osmet did not intend to divulge any more information than was necessary to complete the transaction. But the middle-aged man with stubble on this chin and wearing a bathrobe and slippers appeared even more adamant to know more of his business and wasn't about to release the room key to his possession until he felt satisfied.

"If you must know, sir, I come from Mexico and am on a business trip."

"Why didn't you just fly to your business trip? Or, are you a traveling salesman?"

He sighed heavily; "Please sir, I have driven over two thousand miles and am very tired. Could I please have my room key?"

The motel manager reluctantly handed him the room key and followed him to the office door where he placed the closed sign and locked the door while Osmet walked twenty feet to Room #1. He didn't even bother with taking off his clothes as he fell onto the made bed and fell fast asleep.

Mark woke Hector at 5:30 as he watched the sun rise over the plain of Nebraska. *I can't see a hill for miles*, Mark complained bitterly. *I already miss Washington.*

"Are you ready to go, Hector?"

"Yeah, I'm ready," he yawned loudly and stretched his body that reminded Mark of a lion stretching, as he laid sprawled on his hands and knees stretching his arms and then his legs. He slowly pulled himself off the floor and continued to stretch his back and hips by twisting his torso to and fro, and finally, he bent over, keeping his legs stretched taut while he counted to ten and then went back up straight.

He helped Mark pull the mattresses from the door and window, place them back on the bed frames, and make the beds. Each man then took turns taking showers and shaving. Finally, after they had dressed, they left the room key where the housekeeper would find it, on the bureau between the two beds next to the lamp.

They left the motel and walked together behind the one-story building towards the Dodge Wagon that Hector had made to appear like an abandoned car, with the hood up and the shattered glass back hatch up. Just as they appeared at the car and threw their bags inside, a patrol car pulled up and a police officer wearing a starched khaki uniform, with his shield silver, bright and shiny that reflected off the sun quite nicely, got out from his Chevrolet Caprice.

"Good morning, gentlemen." He had a familiar Midwestern drawl they had become accustomed. "I came out here last night and saw this poor thing sitting all by its lonesome, and for the life of me, couldn't figure why on earth someone would just up and leave this perfectly running vehicle out here behind the motel."

"It's kind of complicated," Mark said to the constable as he tried to shade his eyes from the reflective glare off the badge.

"Well, you see, gentlemen, I have nothing but time on my hands in this fine little town to listen to your complicated tale." The officer turned to one side and spit tobacco juice from a good-sized chew of, what Mark assumed, was Copenhagen.

"We think we're being followed by someone in a black BMW 3i," Mark replied.

The deputy took off his billed cap and scratched his head thoughtfully as he exposed a large bald area where hair once grew. "Where are you coming from?"

"Richland, Washington," Mark replied without hesitation.

"Is this person also from Richland, Washington?"

"We're only speculating at this time," Mark replied, "but we think he's a hired gun from Todos Santos, Mexico, home base of the Lopez Cartel."

"Don't say now," the officer said in such a way that both realized he did not believe a word of it. "I frankly don't give a rat if you are being followed, so long as I don't have to fill out a bunch of reports and such to the district attorney in Lincoln County." He turned around and spit again. "I don't frankly know what to believe, but I would suggest you two move along down the highway and don't come back. Are we clear on this?"

"Chrystal clear," Mark replied as they both got inside the Dodge Aspen and started it up.

"Just out of curiosity, where are you headed?"

"FBI academy in Quantico," Hector replied as Mark placed the wagon into drive and slowly maneuvered from the field and back on the street leading towards the interstate. It was not five minutes later they were cruising at the posted speed limit of 55 miles per hour. Mark did not dare take any chances after their brief encounter with North Platte's finest to go any faster. "So, our next destination is Young Pine, Pennsylvania?" Hector asked.

"Not that I'm aware of," Mark answered. "I believe it's Youngwood, Pennsylvania," Mark corrected. "Go look at the map in the glove box, Hector."

"I took it out last night so that I could see where we were going next. How come you're picking these small towns?"

"So, the map is in your bag then?"

"Yeah, I packed it in my overnight bag after I finished with it last night along with my flashlight that I used."

"To answer your question, it just happened to land that way where the twelve-hundred-mile threshold would be. North Platte happened to be twelve hundred miles from Tri Cities and Youngwood happens to be about twelve hundred miles from North Platte. So, in about twelve hours, or so, we should end up in our next destination. The final leg shouldn't take more than eight hours," Mark explained to his friend as they traveled east on the Nebraska plain.

"But Mark, getting from where you lived to here took over fourteen hours."

"Blame that on the time zone change," Mark reasoned.

Hector nodded.

There's no way I believe that cock and bull story that someone was following those two, the Officer said to himself as he got back inside his cruiser and radioed to dispatch. "The abandoned vehicle report got solved about three minutes ago, Clara."

"What was the hub-bub," the dispatcher called back.

"It seems these two, who were spending the night at the Motel 6, thought they were being followed by someone in a black BMW."

"That's funny John, because Billy Mack and his crew said that some foreigner with a Russian accent wanted them to start a fight last night with some Mexican at the Straw Hat Saloon before that tornado destroyed it. Officer Jones took the report last night when he asked anyone if anything peculiar happened before the tornado touched down. They said this foreign talking guy was driving a black BMW with an odd license plate; something they never seen before."

"Like it was from another country?"

"I don't know. Officer Jones went around town to see if he could find that car, but he never saw it and handed me his report prior to him getting off shift an hour ago."

"Copy that, Clara, out," Officer John Johnson said as he placed the hand mic back on the hook over the radio that sat on top of the dash. *Maybe those boys weren't feeding me a bunch of bull after all.* He went over to the motel and walked inside the office where the manager stood behind a counter. He wore bib overalls and a straw cowboy hat. "Good morning George has your daughter started cleaning yet?"

"That lazy girl," he sneered. "Hell, she's still back there in bed sleeping," he replied scornfully. "Why, what's up?"

"That room you checked two men in last night; one was a Mexican looking guy and the other was a big white guy."

"Yeah, Gonzalez and Marteau; paid with a credit card and everything appeared legit."

"It's not them that are in trouble, George. Can you let me in? I want to check something out."

"Sure, John," the manager replied as he pulled his large key chain full of motel room keys and led the way out the door and walked down the long line of rooms until he came upon room 19. He quickly unlocked the door and let John inside. He glanced inside himself wondering what it was that caused this officer to request this room be opened. "I see I won't need my worthless daughter to clean this room. It doesn't look like it was slept in."

The officer purposely ignored George as he looked inside each drawer of the bureau and on the top of each headboard. He went inside the bathroom and there he spotted a map and a flashlight sitting on top of the toilet. He opened the map and saw his town circled in black as well as Youngwood, Pennsylvania and finally Quantico, Virginia.

He refolded the map, took it with the flashlight, and headed outside to his patrol car. *They might or might not need this, but if they're being followed by this guy, they're driving into a trap.* He grabbed the hand mic and called dispatch. "Clara, how much vacation do I have accumulated?"

"Oh, I'd have to check, but I'm sure it's over a hundred hours."

"I think I have a situation here and I'm going to need to take off for a few days. Do me a favor, Clara. Call Youngwood, PA police and tell them to be on the lookout for a black BMW with foreign license plates, possibly from Baja Mexico. Has the airmail already come and gone?"

"No, it won't land for another hour."

"Good, I'm going to hitch a ride, so I can get to either Omaha or Lincoln."

"That's not SOP you know."

"I know, but I think those boys are in danger and I need to give them a helping hand."

"Do you have any idea of how totally fucked we are right now?" Mark demanded as he watched Hector go through his overnight bag for the fourth time and became increasingly more frustrated while Mark continued to hammer at him.

"I don't understand. I thought for sure I put that map and flashlight in my overnight bag this morning when I finished taking my shower. I laid both the flashlight and the map inside the bag and then I saw my shaving kit was still out. Oh, shit; then I took the map and flashlight out and laid them on the toilet, so I could put them back on top. I'm sorry Bro; I can't believe I left it back at the motel."

Mark sighed heavily as he glared down at his friend. He had choice words to exchange to him, but chose this time, to count slowly to ten as he and Dave always told him to do, and breathe slowly through his nose. After he finished counting, he took a deep breath and exhaled before he said, "It's okay; we'll pick up another map at the next gas station or convenience store we come to."

"It's too bad they haven't invented maps on your cell phone."

"Great, then, instead of losing a five-dollar map, you could lose a two-hundred-dollar cell phone; that would really make my day," Mark replied sarcastically.

"I said I was sorry, man."

"No, I'm sorry I thought this road trip would be halfway successful. Instead, God who knows, has been following us, we had to avoid a tornado and possible bar fight, and now my best friend up and forgets the map. What else could possibly go wrong?"

"The car could break down," Hector replied quietly.

"Hector, don't even say such a thing!" Mark yelled panic-stricken. "We've been so lucky, so far, don't jinx us now."

Mark had pulled into a Nebraska rest stop off Interstate 80. Mark wanted to find the town they would need to start their move south to Interstate 70. The moment Hector saw his toiletry bag on top of his overnight bag, and not the map, he realized the problem.

"The very next town we come to, you're going to buy a map and a marker, and you will circle Youngwood, Pennsylvania, along with Quantico, Virginia."

"Okay, man I got it," Hector replied irked by Mark's relentless assault. He got back in the car and then noticed something else that made his blood turn cold. "Mark, did you fill up last night?"

"No, we got caught in that tornado business, and must've forgotten," Mark replied as he glanced over Hector's shoulder and saw for himself the red gauge indicator was tickling the empty mark. "Son of a bitch," Mark said slowly. "Of course, without a map, we don't know where the next town is, do we? No of course not, Hector because it might be a mile down the road or a hundred!"

"Let's ask around, maybe one of these people here can help us out."

"You go ahead," Mark said with disgust. Hector walked about the rest stop, and did just that, going to the first people he came to.

"Excuse me, do you know how far the next town is?" They were a middle-aged couple on their way to a new job as they had a U-Haul trailer they towed with their Dodge minivan. The man looked at Hector nervously but relaxed a bit when he saw Hector's toothy grin.

"I'm pretty certain Kearney's about ten miles away," the man with short military styled haircut replied. "I take it you're running on empty."

"Yeah, that's putting it mildly," Hector, replied. "I seemed to have misplaced the map too."

"Well, it must suck to be you right now. Have a good one," he called out as he saw Hector turn around and head back to the Dodge Aspen wagon.

"Okay, that guy over there said that Kearney is ten miles away," Hector told Mark in a tone that suggested he wanted this discussion done and over. He got behind the wheel, started the car up as Mark went to the passenger side, and climbed in. They drove down the freeway, not exchanging a word to each other as they both realized this was becoming the longest ten miles of their lives, and Hector kept glancing down at the needle on the fuel gauge.

"Up ahead, I see a Conoco station," Mark said with genuine relief in his voice. Hector pulled up to the pump as it made coughing and sputtering noises before Hector shut off the ignition. Mark filled the tank while Hector paid the attendant and bought some more groceries for their evening meal.

"Here's a map I bought too," Hector told Mark as he got into the passenger side, giving Mark the not so subtle hint, it was his turn to drive. Mark took an extra second to check under the hood, making sure everything checked out before they continued their road trip.

Once Mark was satisfied, he closed the hood and got behind the wheel and started the car up, placed the shifter into drive and drove back out onto the freeway-merging lane.

"How much further to the first interchange that we come to?" Mark asked Hector in a no-non-sense manner that suggested his angst had passed.

He studied the map briefly before he replied, "Outside Omaha is the closest and it goes south."

"That works for me," Mark said. "I'm sorry I got so heated earlier; shit happens, and I got frustrated."

"I was mad at myself too dude. I should have double-checked to make sure your map got back in my overnight bag. And my flashlight that I've had since I was a young recruit in Basic."

"What's the name of the interstate we need to get on?"

"Interstate 29 to Kansas City, and then we'll be on I-70 going east."

"That's what I want; thank you, Hector."

"Can you believe how much wheat and corn fields there are out here? It's no wonder they call this the 'bread basket of the world.'"

"I'm sure if you guys didn't have a bunch of drug lords ruling and ruining your country, you could have that claim to fame too."

"We did have that kind of claim to fame, amigo. I don't know what happened, but suddenly the peon farmers got cheated or thrown off their ancestral lands, and cocoa and marijuana plants inundated the landscape, which, would have been fine had pot and coke been legal, but it ain't."

Mark did not say any more about it, but he secretly wondered if there was a conspiracy afoot. The drive proved uneventful as they arrived at the I-29 interchange and headed south. They crossed the Missouri River into the state of Missouri and continued to the next interchange in Kansas City and headed east on I-70. Missouri went from flat plains to more rolling hills and woodlands the further east they traveled until the familiar Arch that designated the St Louis skyline appeared as it approached 5 o'clock.

Hector took over the driving as they fueled up the car and ate tacos they cooked up from a skillet and cook stove at the Silver Lake Rest area in western Illinois. Farmland and woodland interspersed with small and medium sized towns to create a tapestry of Americana at its finest.

As far as Mark was concerned, these places were where Ronald Reagan and Dwight Eisenhower were idolized, and the Kennedys were demonized. *Why they could not win the war on drugs escapes me*, Mark said to himself. *I guess though, they would not be hiring people like us to become FBI agents if they'd won.*

They drove through Indiana, and then Ohio as darkness slowly materialized over the area. They finally crossed the Pennsylvania border after nine o'clock and Hector looked down at the road map to see how much further to Youngwood, they needed to go. "It looks like another hour and we should be there," Hector told Mark, who nodded at his friend.

A sign suddenly came into view warning drivers the Pennsylvania Turnpike was a mile away. "Get your money out, amigo; we got a toll to pay."

After paying the toll, they proceeded to New Stanton and went up Highway 119 to South 3rd Street. Hector and Mark looked hard for a motel but found nothing, but a colonial looking bed and breakfast called Youngwood Cottage. They pulled into the front of the house and went inside to register, where they just happened to spot that same police officer from North Platte, Nebraska, dressed in blue jeans, checkered buttoned-down shirt and straw cowboy hat propped on top of his bald head. He sat casually on a couch in the lobby. He smiled at them

"What the hell are you doing here?" Mark asked accusingly, though not meaning to.

"I think I've come to save you twos' hides," he replied. "I got word before I left what went down at the Straw Hat Saloon before that tornado struck. I also got information on your friend, at least as much as Inter-Pol would divulge to me. Your friend is a former Agent from the Yugoslavian Security Service, who now works for a Che Lopez down in Mexico, but I'm sure you already know that part of the equation."

"I take it then that you know this would be our next stop before we made it down to Quantico, Virginia," Mark said. "And, that if you know this, then that asshole knows this too."

"His name is Osmet Vuk, an assassin with a way of getting the job done quietly and efficiently," John went on to say. "Here's your map and flashlight. My thought is that with the three of us, he may get discouraged and not want to carry out this business."

"I like your way of thinking," Mark said. "But, we pretty much planned for such a contingency. We both have our personal weapons and know how to use them."

"Then, you wouldn't mind a third gun then, would you?"

"Not at all," Hector replied. "I'm glad to have you on board." Hector noticed Mark's less than happy expression on this, but Mark said nothing, realizing too that three against one had the odds more in their favor than his.

"I take it that you already have a room here?" Mark asked the officer.

"Yeah, I booked a room about two hours ago when I flew in here. I didn't realize how small a town this was until I got off the plane and asked the taxi driver about it. This is the only hotel in town; everything else is over in New Stanton, a little bit bigger town, I gathered. My name is John Johnson by the way, and you two?"

"I'm Mark Marteau and this is Hector Gonzalez."

"Yeah, that Osmet character knows human nature quite well," Officer Johnson, said. "He went up to a group of farm boys that really don't like strangers with brown skin and Spanish surnames. One of my officers asked after the tornado hit the Straw Hat Saloon about anything peculiar prior, and them boys confessed about that Osmet guy offering them five thousand dollars to beat you to death."

"We had a feeling about that too," Hector agreed. "The moment they walked inside and spotted me, I saw something wasn't right. God was definitely on my side yesterday," he said as he crossed himself.

"That's when we decided to take our chances by getting out of there. Rather than go down that storm shelter, we hid inside our motel room, parking the car out in that back field to let that guy think we left," Mark continued.

"I must say, your quick thinking definitely kept you two alive so far. I come here to make sure that you make it the rest of the way. Go ahead and check in. I'll buy you two a couple of beers and then we'll make an early start of it tomorrow morning."

Osmet waited patiently on the junction where Highway 119 and the I-70 occurred. He purposefully kept out of sight as he watched for the Dodge Wagon to appear. He waited at this spot since 7 o'clock and wondered if maybe they had car troubles, when he spotted the car drive pass with the Mexican driving towards the town of Youngwood. *I will follow them*, he said to himself as he started the BMW and shifted into first and slowly came up behind them from twenty meters away and stopped.

Osmet saw the car stop and watched them get out from the wagon, heading to a house that he could only speculate was a hostel. He waited and then saw them leave with another man. "Who is this?" He quickly called Che to inform him.

"What news have you brought me, Osmet?" Che answered the phone, possibly expecting to hear some good news of an accomplished deed.

"I'm in a small town in Pennsylvania called Youngwood. It appears a new player has joined the party, Senor Lopez."

"Interesting," Che replied. "I will pay you five thousand more to take care of him too. I do not know how this one came about, but we do not want any loose ends."

"I understand," Osmet, said as he received the green light that he hoped for from Che. "It will be taken care of tonight."

"Very good, then I hope to hear from you tomorrow morning at 8."

"It will be done," Osmet replied as he disconnected the call by flipping the phone closed.

He slowly made his way around the bed and breakfast until he reached the back door. It appeared unlocked and he allowed himself inside. He pulled out a small flashlight from his suit pocket and shined it in the vicinity, trying to gauge exactly what room he had found himself. *It is their scullery*, he surmised. He saw all the utensils, along with pots and pans hanging from hooks over chopping blocks and long stainless-steel counters. He searched other rooms until he found the furnace room located in a cellar, downstairs. He examined the furnace and saw it had recently been converted to natural gas from coal. He saw the coal dust on the floor. *It doesn't matter to me how many innocents passed tonight, so long as my job is done.* He noticed the furnace was off because it being summer, there was no need, though the pilot light remained on.

This will be very easy, he said to himself. He checked his wristwatch and the LED showed it to be after 10:30. *Everyone should be in bed by now, even Mr. Marteau and his two accomplices.* Osmet proceeded to blow out the pilot light and turned on the valve releasing the natural gas. He then made his way outside. *Unless they are very light sleepers, the gas will suffocate them, or better yet, a habitual smoker could do the trick too when he or she lights up their cigarette.*

Mark, Hector and John arrived back to the bed and breakfast some fifteen minutes later and went inside the house that Mark thought might have been around since the 1700s. Mark and Hector did not appear to notice the slight but pungent odor of rotten eggs that whipped up, but John, having lived in the Midwest, recognized the smell immediately and yelled, "Gas!"

"What, gas?" Mark asked confused by this man's sudden outburst.

"Quick, get everyone out of here; there's a gas leak in this place coming from somewhere," John ordered the two as he went across the street and used his cell phone to call 911.

"I smell it now," Hector said as he sniffed the air. "It smells like adjetivo huevos."

They ran to every room on the main floor, as well as upstairs and were able to get everyone out, even the old cranky owner.

"To think, I got the best sleep in years and it's due to a gas leak," she complained bitterly. The local volunteer fire department arrived ten minutes later.

After everyone had gathered across the street, Mark and Hector both heard it and could not understand why someone would be calling the bed and breakfast at this hour. They remembered it was a black rotary phone with a handle that sat on the cradle and looked so ancient that Mark appreciated it because of its nostalgic appearance. The sudden, resulting explosion was so intense, windows shattered for miles around when the old wooden structure disintegrated before their eyes. The blast knocked everyone down and the exposed gas line shot up a long four-foot high flame until the gas company shut off the main valve on 3rd Street.

Hector and Mark picked themselves off the ground, along with everyone else as they flicked off their scorched eyebrows and silently prayed that they made it out alive.

"That son of a bitch," Mark screamed. "He's going to pay for this."

"It was a gas leak, Mark," Hector tried to explain to his angry friend.

"The hell it was," Mark replied, "that was just too coincidental to be anything other than an attempt at taking us out." He fumed as he saw the rubble that was a bed and breakfast lying strewn over a six-hundred-foot radius. The blast started smaller fires and the one engine that arrived had sustained significant damage as well as Mark's Dodge wagon that appeared blackened and the side windows blown out.

"Let's get out of here," Mark said as he went to his car, got in behind the wheel, and started it up. The other two followed, not certain what Mark had in mind, as they brushed the glass fragments off their seats before getting in too.

Mark pulled away, went back toward New Stanton, and arrived at the Express Inn. They got their rooms and went to bed not saying another word until the next morning.

They all three went to the continental breakfast being served in an alcove just off from the lobby that overlooked the parking lot. "I trust everyone slept well last night," Mark stated over a heaping plate of toast and a cup of coffee.

Naturally, the place appeared busy as at least a dozen other guests came down to grab a quick bite before going their separate ways. Conversations and other subtle noises of silverware clattering against cheap ceramic cups and saucers, competed with Mark's greeting to his partners.

"Yeah, for the most part, Mark," Hector replied as he picked through the fruit plate.

"I just didn't realize that rascal knew where we were staying," John said bewildered by last night's experience. "Are your weapons still in your possession," he asked in a hushed tone so only they could hear. Both nodded as Mark replied, "They're under the front seat," using a slightly higher tone as someone called out for more muffins just as Mark started to speak. "That's one of the reasons I decided to leave, figuring they would have to search my car and didn't want to answer a bunch of questions."

"I take it neither of you two have registered hand guns?"

"No, because I am a law-abiding citizen and don't think I need to pay them government assholes for my right to bear arms," Mark replied.

"I just never got around to it," Hector replied honestly.

"Well my firearm was inside that bed and breakfast, and I will have to buy a new one."

"That might be hard to do with background checks and all," Mark said bitterly. "Goddamn government always looking for ways to take away our rights, one law at a time."

"Mark, you forget, I'm in law enforcement, and I'm exempt from the waiting period. I'll show you as soon as I call home and tell them what happened. They will fax me a writ over to whatever firearms dealer or pawn shop there is in this town. I'll wait maybe as long as it takes for that fax to arrive."

"I knew there was a reason I joined the FBI," Mark said, as he just happened to glance outside and saw a familiar looking car parked in front of a room. "Look guys, isn't that the BMW?"

"I don't know Mark, you tell us," Hector replied.

"I suggest you take my car, John and get yourself a gun like right now," Mark said with slow determination.

"You got it," John replied as he took the keys from Mark's hands and quickly left the lobby. Mark and Hector saw John get inside the half-scorched Dodge wagon and leave the lot.

Osmet slept in later than he planned, but felt he deserved such a sweet pleasure considering his targets were no longer around and he felt twenty-five thousand dollars richer. *There is a pool here; I think I will go for a swim this morning and call Che and tell him the good news.* Normally he would confirm his success, but after feeling and seeing the explosion from his rearview mirror and seeing all those fire trucks streaming by with their lights and sirens, he did not feel he had to. *The phone call I made, was a nice bit of drama too*, he mused to himself. He pulled out his own guilty pleasure and took a deep drag from the Camel unfiltered cigarette.

He changed to a swimsuit he always packed in his suitcase for such an occasion. He went out to the pool and dove in immediately swimming several laps, before pulling himself up from the pool and drying himself off with a white terry cloth towel. *I might just decide to drive to Philadelphia and take a plane back to Mexico,* Osmet said to himself. *I am sure some poor black man would have good use for such a car. I can always buy another when I get to Todos Santos. This country is much too big for one to drive such a distance.* He had his back to the parking lot and didn't see the Dodge wagon suddenly leave.

Osmet went back inside his room and took a long shower to wash off the three days of stench that accumulated on his body. After he had dressed in a clean suit, he called Che on his cell phone. "I have wonderful news, Che. Your two enemies are dead, along with whoever their friend was," he told the Mexican drug lord in Spanish.

"And you have confirmation of this, Osmet?"

"Well I saw the explosion when the gas ignited from the hotel they stayed at last night."

"That isn't what I asked, my friend. You will need to go back and confirm they are all dead, and then I will pay you."

"Very well, Che," Osmet replied not hiding his frustration. "I will cut off each of their ears as proof and send them to you." He disconnected the call before Che could reply.

He got inside his car and went back to Youngwood where many police and fire investigators converged on the heap of rubble that was a bed and breakfast. *How could anyone come out of that alive?* He took a picture using the cell phone's rudimentary camera that seemingly took, at best a very fuzzy facsimile of the image he was trying to capture. *Maybe, one day they will make better cameras for these cell phones*, he said to himself as he looked at the picture he took and stored it in his phone for Che to see for himself when he returned.

Osmet drove away slowly to not garner attention as he made his way back onto the freeway and headed east towards Philadelphia. He did not think to look out his rear-view mirror as he drove the speed limit and paid more attention to the West Pennsylvania countryside of rolling hills and forests that reminded him so much of his beloved Serbia. He never saw the half-scorched Dodge Aspen Wagon slowly but steadily gaining on him.

Mark had no experience going after someone and Hector didn't want to be accused of wrecking another one of Mark's cars, so John took the wheel when he returned from the pawn shop in New Stanton toting a sawed-off shotgun. "I showed him my badge and the pawn broker told me that they received a shipment of old shotguns from some small-town police station that closed up shop. He said, 'you don't need to fill anything out and you're exempt because you have that badge there.' I liked him; he's definitely one of us."

Mark took over the passenger seat and sat next to John, and Hector sat behind Mark as they sped out of there and Mark stated, "That asshole took off about ten minutes ago. I'm thinking this Lopez guy probably wants proof he killed us last night."

"It wouldn't surprise me any," John replied as he headed back towards Youngwood. They stopped at a traffic light when they saw the black BMW make a left turn, driving onto the I-70 turnpike heading east. John suddenly cut someone off, receiving an angry honk from the driver's horn, as he turned right and followed the black car. "You let me do the driving, boys. When we get to a spot where I can get him pulled over, safely, then we can take care of business. The main thing about this is we can't get other people involved, unless maybe the state police."

"Frankly, I wouldn't even want them involved," Mark said as he fished out his and Hector's holsters, placing his over his shoulder, while passing Hector's to him, and he strapped his Colt .45 to his hip. Mark opened his chambers to ensure the revolver had six rounds, while Hector slid back the receiver pushing a fresh round into the chamber and placing the .45 back into his holster.

They caught up to the BMW after about twenty miles. John saw him cruising at around sixty-five miles per hour. Traffic, though not particularly heavy, was steady and John feared it would be too dangerous to risk here. Suddenly the black car sped up, but John stayed on him. "I think he just saw us and realized we're not dead after all," John noted.

"It must suck to be him right now," Hector said with a smirk.

I do not believe my eyes, Osmet said to himself with uncertainty in his heart. He accelerated his BMW to see how this American made car would handle this jaunt. To his chagrin, the older car kept up and he saw the driver was not Mark or the Mexican, but this new person, whom he had never seen, but who appeared much more experienced driving like this.

Osmet's car accelerated past 90 miles per hour, yet the Dodge stayed on track. Osmet realized he needed to get off this freeway and be more within his element. He took the Clay Pike exit and drove quickly up the road until he saw Freeman Falls Road, but that pesky Dodge wagon stayed right on his heels.

Finally, he took Rock Oak Lane and took an abrupt turn stopping at the roundabout and pulling out his personal Zastava M70 semi-automatic pistol, fired wildly at the car as if it was possessed.

John stopped the car as soon as he saw the tall, slender man with pencil thin mustache appear from the BMW brandishing his gun and firing at them. He pulled out the shotgun, loaded with 00 buckshot and fired back when it malfunctioned. However, the one round he fired did hit its mark, hitting Osmet's upper thigh, putting him down with blood trickling from his pants leg.

Mark opened his car door as he saw Osmet aim his pistol at John, who was attempting to do an immediate action by pumping the shotgun to discharge the empty round. Mark returned fire, hitting Osmet's shooting arm with such force it knocked his gun to the ground.

Hector came up and around Mark. He walked purposefully to his target, fired three rounds into his torso and head, killing the assassin.

"Is everyone okay?" John asked as he watched Mark and Hector holstered their handguns, and inspected the dead assassin who lay sprawled on the ground. Both men stared at the corpse and John wondered just how cold blooded these two were when he saw them both bow their heads praying silently and Hector crossing himself.

"We're fine," Mark replied quietly. "What do we do now?"

John knew the right thing to do would be to call in the police and any other number of state agencies that would handle this, costing these boys time they most likely didn't have. He looked around him and saw miles and miles of woodland and hills.

"You boys need to get to Quantico; I'll take care of our friend here. Just do me a favor and don't say anything to anyone about what happened here. Are we clear on that?"

"Crystal," Mark replied.

"Go on your way now and be the best damn FBI agents this country has ever seen," John told them. He went up to the corpse of Osmet Vuk and pulled him inside the BMW's passenger side front seat and placed his straw hat over Osmet's head hiding the bullet hole and made it appear that he was taking a nap while John drove him to wherever in this keystone state.

1991

A year later, after Che had all but given up hope Osmet would ever show up, he received a package from a Federal Express van on a sunny and warm autumn day. The package came from Somerset, Pennsylvania and it looked like a perfectly cubed box that had the word perishable stamped on the front with a PO Box and Osmet's name as a returned address.

Did he finally show me the proof I needed to have complete peace of mind? Che quickly opened the package inside his office and looked inside the box. Suddenly he dropped the box and let out a terrified scream, heard throughout the mansion when he discovered what was inside; Osmet's decapitated head rolled out of the box and onto the floor.

October 15, 2014

"Hey Hector," Mark called out to his friend as they traveled toward Missoula Airport. "Ever wonder whatever happened to old John Johnson?"

"I'm sure wherever or whatever he's doing, he's plenty happy about it; he's the kind of guy that's at peace no matter what."

END

MYSTERY AT THE OLD AMERICAN LEGION BUILDING

October 15, 2014

Mark and Hector spotted Missoula Airport. To Mark it appeared about the same size as the airport in Spokane; perhaps a little smaller. It was after all, the largest airport due to Missoula being a college town and the second largest city in Montana.

Mark's mind drifted back to the FBI Academy and all the bullshit he had to learn and earn his bachelor's degree in Criminal Justice from UVC to complete his requirement to become an FBI agent. Therefore, by that early December day in 1990, he was ready for his first field office assignment.

This then took Mark and Hector back to the airliner at Dulles Airport that would take them to Spokane. Just as this airport was going to send them down to Todos Santos Mexico to confront Che Lopez or whoever else one last time.

December 6, 1990

Mark hoped that Hector would be assigned at the same field office, though he already made his preference known at the academy that he wanted somewhere warm and dry. To Mark's pleasant surprise and Hector's chagrin, they received the same assignment at Spokane, Washington.

"This is all your fault," Hector told Mark as they boarded the plane going from Washington's Dulles Airport on a drizzly December evening.

"How can it be my fault, Hector?"

"I don't know but somehow or some way God is pissed at me and he's got me sentenced to you for the rest of my life."

"I thought you wanted to be with me."

"Shit, dream on amigo. I figured you'd want a new occupation and that's why I sent you that letter. I didn't expect to be your friggin sidekick from here on out."

Mark and Hector reported to Joe Armstrong on December 8, 1990 at the Washington, Idaho and Montana district office amid little fanfare. The only thing they looked forward to, and Mark felt thrown totally off guard from when Joe interviewed him eight months ago, was how much of an asshole Joe had become.

They walked into the office where Mark and Hector reported for their first assignment, both were dressed in the business suits of the time as the instructors warned Mark he wouldn't be allowed to wear his throwback suits, at least not until after he established a rapport with the station chief. However, when he saw Joe would be his boss, he relaxed his anxious demeanor and offered his hand to Special Agent Armstrong.

"What the hell are you doing Marteau? I'm not your long loss cousin at a family reunion. I'm your boss and if for one moment you think that we're buddies, you have another thing coming."

Mark immediately dropped his hand and stood at rigid attention, along with Hector Gonzalez who glared at his friend from the corner of his eye. "I'm sorry sir, it won't happen again," Mark replied.

"Apparently, you thought we were friends when I interviewed you for this job. That couldn't be further from the truth, Agent Marteau. Right now, you and Agent Gonzalez are probationary agents; what we like to call probies. You will remain such for the better part of a year. After which you will be given your marching orders to either go to a new assignment or stay here with me for another year. Am I making myself clear so far?"

"Yes Sir," both men replied.

"Right now, you're in luck; we got handed a case in which we'll be assisting the Spokane Police

Department. A janitor and security guard came upon a body of a nude ten-year-old girl—a Jane Doe—lying in the morgue."

Mark's appearance hadn't changed a bit, except for not being allowed to wear his beloved retro-look suits from any estate sale or local Goodwill thrift stores that carried them. Hector on the other hand had decided to grow a mustache, for which Mark made a point of giving him unending grief. "Sir are there any policies concerning facial growth on FBI agents," Mark asked with a sheepish grin.

Joe looked at Hector's attempt at a mustache that was black and quite thin and trimmed, well within the standards for facial hair and then he saw Mark's grin, as if he wanted to start something, while he noticed Hector glaring at him. "I find nothing wrong with your partner's mustache, Agent Marteau. I suggest if you want to continue giving your partner grief over his appearance, you check yourself in the mirror first. Your hair needs grooming, Agent Marteau."

"Yes Sir," Mark replied as he quickly started to leave his supervisor's office.

"Where are you going, Marteau? I haven't released you yet," Agent Armstrong demanded.

"Sorry Sir, it won't happen again."

"See that it doesn't. Back to the Jane Doe case; according to the medical examiner's pre-autopsy report, her c.o.d. was blunt force trauma to her head. There were several lacerations and contusions all over her body, suggesting she may have fallen, or she might have been pushed; perhaps down a flight of stairs."

Hector took notes while Mark looked about his boss' office, seemingly paying little attention to what Agent Armstrong told him. He yawned noticeably, and a look of total disinterest crossed his face.

"Agent Marteau is there something wrong?"

"Not at all, sir; I was just wondering if we get weekends off?"

"Are you fucking serious? I'm here debriefing you on your first homicide investigation, and you want to know about weekends?"

"Sorry sir," Mark replied sincerely. "It's just I haven't seen my parents in six months and would like to go down there and see them."

"Agent Marteau, if you continue to ask stupid questions like that, I'll make it a point to send you home to visit your parents permanently. Do I make myself clear?" Joe Armstrong asked in a clearly controlled rage.

"Yes sir," Mark replied tersely. "So, the theory so far is that she either fell down a flight of stairs or was pushed. Can we go to the crime scene?"

"Of course, Agent Marteau" the station chief replied evenly. "As a matter of fact, I want you two to visit the crime scene and the police investigators-- their names are Marcus and Anthony-- to glean anything new. Here's the address." He handed Hector the printed-out sheet of paper that Mark snatched from his hand and handed back to

Hector. "We're working together on this, so we're sharing everything connected to this investigation," Joe Armstrong concluded.

Mark appeared uncomfortable by this but did not say anything on that point. "Are we released then?"

"Yes, now you are released. I want a report on today's activities on my desk before you leave tonight at eight."

"Eight?" Mark asked in disbelief. "But, it's eight now; you mean we have to work twelve hours?"

"Remember me telling you about any more stupid questions, Agent Marteau?"

"Yes sir," Mark replied like a disciplined child. They headed out the office and found their desks inside a cubicle with two other desks, besides Hector's.

"Dude, you have got to chill," Hector admonished Mark. "I don't know what you were trying to do in there, but he was about ready to send you your walking papers."

"I don't understand it," he replied in disbelief. "I thought he liked me."

"This ain't summer camp. This is the real world, and right now, we have a real investigation to help solve. So, I would suggest you put away your aw-shucks attitude and put on your professional hat and get busy."

Mark heard what he said but didn't like how his first day was going and wanted to have a heart to heart with Joe Armstrong to try to clear the air but realized now wasn't the time. Mark sat down at his desk, looking at the Hewitt Packard terminal and monitor sitting in front of him. He looked at the agents' handbook, rifled through the pages until he found the login protocol, punched in the keys, and created his personal password.

The system came to life while the monitor fed Mark a mess of numerals and words until the screen to the FBI database appeared. Mark then had to create a username and another password; he used the same password to login to the database, and then he saw the screen that he needed to get started.

Hector stared at him in disbelief when he stated, "You know I don't believe Agent Armstrong wanted you to be an armchair investigator."

"I know that, Hector. But it won't hurt to at least have this thing up and running. Then, we'll go to the crime scene and then talk to those Spokane detectives. After that, I want to do what we were taught at academy; some forensic analysis to see if there is a similar pattern here."

"That sounds reasonable," Hector agreed as he too went to his terminal and logged in to the system. That's when Special Agent Armstrong came by the cubicle and stopped in his tracks, when he asked in disbelief, "What the hell are you two doing?"

"We were going to get into the system now, so when we come back we can do some forensic analysis to find similar patterns," Hector replied with anxious tone as if he got caught in the cookie jar.

"I want you two on the streets investigating, now!" Agent Armstrong stormed away from the cubicle just as two other agents walked in. One appeared about Mark's size, but slightly paunchier and older with shaved head, though Mark could see he would be mostly bald anyway and a sizeable handlebar mustache. The other could have been considered a dwarf and to Mark, had to have received some sort of exemption for height and weight, as he barely reached past five feet and couldn't have weighed more than 90 pounds. Yet he carried himself with the confidence of a man twice as large.

"Well then, I see our probies are here to make Joe Armstrong take his hypertension medication," the short man with black curly hair and wicked looking sideburns that Mark could only dream of having before he changed his appearance back in 1977, said in an accent that reminded him of New England and Ivy Leaguers.

"I don't understand why he is so pissed off," Mark stated in exasperation.

"Don't worry about it," the big guy stated. "He does that more for show than anything. I'm Bob Smith and this is my partner, Howard Jones."

Mark and Hector shook both their hands, exchanging their names and smiling sincerely while in the back of Mark's mind Mark wondered, *Can I trust these two?*

Hector asked Special Agent Jones, "How did you get exempt on the height and weight minimums?"

"It helps to have a PhD in Criminal psychology," Howard answered with all the certainty of a seasoned veteran. He had a clipped New England accent that reminded Mark of Maine Lobster and Boston Red Sox games.

"Are you like a profiler then," Mark asked in awe.

"In a manner of speaking, yes," Howard Jones replied.

"What can you enlighten us on this Jane Doe case we just got so far?" Mark asked referring to the present investigation.

Howard shook his head as he jumped on his office chair, purposefully rose to the highest level and replied, "It's been too long. What trace evidence we gathered and sent to the lab at Quantico is so old and possibly contaminated I don't think we could glean anything from it that could possibly lead to a suspect, let alone how she died."

"The police, on the lead of the security guard and janitor who found her outside the American Legion Building. We think it could have been in that dumpster over three days, and the medical examiner confirmed that hypothesis." Special Agent Smith continued when he took a sip from a coffee mug with an E.W.U. logo pasted on the outer part of the mug in the shape of a red eagle. "It definitely looked like someone either pushed her, or she fell somewhere. The city detectives haven't found out where yet."

"Then we're probably dealing with a cold case that may never get solved," Mark said with a bitter attitude.

"That's why the police asked us to come on board," Bob Smith replied. "I would suggest that you keep that negativity locked up in a closet somewhere deep inside your brain too, probie.

"That's the last thing you need when trying to solve a murder investigation; keep plugging away and always have a smile on your face even after you've been on your twelfth hour of the twenty-ninth straight day and you haven't seen your wife and kids in over a month."

"Well, I don't have to worry about that," Mark stated enthusiastically. "I'm not married."

"You're not?" Howard Jones asked in a come-hither manner as he winked knowingly at Mark to get a rise out of him.

"And I ain't gay neither," Mark yelled garnering laughs from all three men. "Well I suppose we better get down to the crime scene and talk to the lead detective on this, Hector."

"It's on the corner of Riverside and Washington," Bob volunteered.

Both men left Bob and Howard, went to the fleet dispatch, signed out for 1990 Ford Crown Victoria and drove up Riverside. It was one of the few streets in downtown Spokane that had two-way traffic.

"Do you know where we're going, amigo?" Hector asked his partner as they approached Washington.

"Well, the address is 108 South Washington, and I think right here is the building with the columns and pitched roof," Mark replied as he made a left turn on Washington and pulled into the back-parking lot, where crime scene tape was strewn around the dumpster and a fifty-foot diameter zone to keep civilians away.

"This is typical of French Renaissance Revival-style," Mark told Hector.

"It was a popular method for buildings of the early 1900s era– such as the hipped roof, reminiscent of French Chateauesque-style influences, Minnesota sandstone, blond pressed brick veneer and cream-colored terra cotta facades."

"How do you know that?"

"My dad was really into that stuff and I guess it rubbed off on me. I think he wanted me to be like him; or even go into architecture so I could follow his example.

"What really looks unique, I think, is the inset loggia with its colossal columns and Corinthian capitals on the west side," Mark concluded that gave Hector pause while he stared at his partner unable to come up with a reply.

"I noticed the sixth floor's light is on. To me, Mark, this place seems eviler and more sinister than historic; looks like I'm seeing a one eyed black cat. I don't think I've ever seen a building like this before," Hector stated as they both braced them-selves for the cold blast of arctic air. "Remind me again why you made me choose this place to start our career as FBI agents?"

"You are such a pussy," Mark replied as he ran to the dumpster and pulled out his notepad and pen from his inner coat pocket with his gloved right hand.

"I never thought you could move that fast," Hector yelled after him as he followed close behind. "How cold is it anyway?"

"I heard the weather man say it was in the teens today. It feels ten times colder with this wind, though."

"All I know is it ain't this cold down in LA right now."

Mark shrugged his shoulders as he cut the seal to the dumpster lid and opened it up, showing an empty container. "Was it empty when they found her?"

"I have no idea," Hector replied as he took notes of that. "I guess we go inside and look around."

"What, you don't want to enjoy this beautiful autumn day?"

"Do you?"

"Yeah, I guess you're right, let's go inside." Mark resealed the container with his own tape, initialing and dating when it was resealed. Then they moved swiftly inside the building and the first thing Mark noticed was how well preserved the interior looked. What floors were not already carpeted, had highly polished, glass-like tiles. In front of the elevators stood the business directory; most appeared vacant, and the few that were occupied, had a pair of doctors and an attorney, and on the top floor, The Taj Import & Export Company. "Let's see what these guys know," Mark suggested.

Mark and Hector went inside an Otis Elevator that could very well been the original as Hector pushed the "Closed" button, watching the two doors close, and Mark pushed the well-worn 6 floor button.

They arrived to see a double door with frosted glass windows that gave only a cursory impression of shapes inside with a black block-lettered sign that read Taj Import/Exports Company. Hector attempted to open the locked door. He tapped on the window of the door.

"It doesn't appear anyone is home," Mark reasoned.

"Maybe they don't come in until later," Hector added as he stepped back being readied to leave, when the tumblers of the door caught, and a man poked his head out. He had the appearance of someone from Eastern Europe. He had a round face, a long thin nose, piercing brown eyes, and he wore a high fur hat worn by Russians that instantly gave Mark an uneasy feeling.

"May I help you," he asked in an Eastern European accent, though neither Mark nor Hector could pinpoint where.

Both men pulled their credentials and announced simultaneously, "FBI, we are here to ask you some questions concerning a body found in the dumpster two days ago.

His smile, a thin sinister looking grin that appeared more like a snarl than a smile, sent a shiver down Mark's spine as he took an instant disliking to the man. "I saw police investigating dumpster, but I have nothing to tell you."

"Can we come in?" Mark asked as he reached in his coat pocket to grab his notepad and pen.

"Only if you have warrant," he replied frostily.

"May we have your name then?" Hector asked with a determined voice.

"My name is Brateslav Manovich."

"What can you tell us," Mark asked with a hint of impatience in his voice.

"Sir, I only know what I saw two days ago. Your city police had my parking spot barricaded and they looked inside dumpster full of trash."

"Are you certain the dumpster was full?" Mark asked.

"I can only assume, sir. Now if you excuse me, I must go."

"I thank you for your time Mr. Manovich," Hector said as he tapped Mark on the shoulder to let Brateslav Manovich pass.

Mark reluctantly moved out of his way as he went toward the elevator after closing and locking the door. "A bit of a sour puss if you ask me," Mark stated as he saw Manovich get on the elevator and watched the numerals flash down a horizontal line to the main floor. "I don't like him," Mark stated bluntly.

"Yeah, he gave me pause too. I'm not going to go as far as saying I don't like him. It's just I don't know; I guess I just don't trust him for some reason," Hector replied. "And it's not just the way he acted towards us just now; there's something else about him that isn't jibing with me."

Mark nodded as he nonchalantly grabbed the doorknob to presumably ensure it was locked. Then he reached inside his coat, pulled out a roll of movers' tape, and taped over the doorknob, and finally pulling the tape off the knob. He then pulled out a sandwich bag from his coat pocket, placed the tape inside, and sealed the bag, placing that back inside his coat pocket. "We're done here, Hector; let's go talk to the city detectives next."

After being lost and turned around and lost again, they finally located the building where the detective bureau stood just up from the county courthouse off Mallon. Neither Mark nor Hector took the time to marvel at the structure's architectural elegance as the wind cut through their coats with such abandon, they felt like icicles after they ran inside.

It appeared like the inside of any modern office design, as a maze of cubicles spread across the main floor and a couple of actual offices stood off to the side. It appeared most of the detectives were out on other cases, as only a handful could be seen either at their desks talking on their phones or typing their reports on the terminals' keyboards.

Mark walked up to the first person he saw behind a desk, typing in the traditional hunt and peck method, seemingly frustrated by his own carelessness. "Excuse me, detective," Mark announced to the red-faced man who seemed lost in trying to find the key to spell out a correct word on his report.

"What do you want?" He asked trying hard to ignore the intruder.

"I'm looking for either Detective Marcus or Detective Anthony," Agent Marteau replied with a neutral tone.

"What do you want with them two assholes?" The detective asked still focused more on the twenty-eight keys on the keyboard, finally finding that key and punching it onto the green screen.

"I'm Agent Marteau and Agent Gonzales from the FBI. I understand they are lead investigators of the body found in the dumpster at 108 South Washington?""

"I want to see some identification first before I show you where they are," he replied in a brusque tone that set both men on edge, but they pulled out their credentials anyway and showed them to him. Satisfied, he jerked his thumb behind his back, "Their name plates are on the outside cubicle about twenty feet that way."

"Thank you," Mark said as he and Hector took the detective's direction and headed twenty feet to a set of cubicles with nameplate Jo Marcus and Carol Anthony stenciled neatly. The two women were on the phone and their conversations were hushed and cryptic with "I see", "uhha" and "What would be a good time to meet?" going on. They both appeared to be oblivious to Mark and Hector's presence.

After about five minutes, they both hung up about the same time and noticed the two FBI agents for the first time. Neither woman was very young, but somewhere in their mid-thirties with average good looks that Mark characterized as career path women not interested in getting married types.

"Can I help you?" Jo asked the two men first as she wiped back a strand of brown hair that hung over her left eye just after hanging up the phone in a memorized manner without taking her eyes off Mark. She seemed to eye Mark provocatively as if asking for his number with body language and giving Hector no more than a passing glance.

"I'm FBI Agent Mark Marteau and my partner is Agent Hector Gonzales. We have been assigned to the murder investigation about that Jane Doe girl found in the dumpster."

"That is such a shame too," Carol Anthony chimed in. "She looked so pretty and innocent. I want to find the person who did it and make sure he pays for what he did."

"Did you guys talk with any of the business owners in that building to see if they might have seen something," Hector asked the two women detectives.

"No, not yet; we first wanted to get the autopsy results from the medical examiner before we started questioning the tenants," Jo replied still giving Mark a thorough going over. "Are you seeing anyone?"

"What? No, I'm not," Mark, replied looking uncomfortable and causing Hector to stifle a belly laugh with a loud cough. "Well, we had an opportunity to talk with a Mr. Brateslav Manovich. He seemed genuinely impressed by our legal system and refused to let us in without a search warrant. I almost had the impression he had something to hide."

"What business did he come from," Jo asked, as her brown eyes seem to show doe-like at Mark.

"Taj Import/Export Company," Mark replied quickly trying to advert his eyes from hers and blushing noticeably.

"We should discuss this case more tonight Agent Marteau—say over cocktails and dinner at Anthony's Seafood. You like seafood, don't you Mark?"

"Yes, no…I mean, can we get on with the case?" He cried desperately.

"It's okay. Meet us at Anthony's sometime around seven and fill us in on this Brat, whatever," Jo said in a husky sounding voice that dripped honey and lavender. She seemed to fiddle with the top button of her white cotton blouse.

Mark swallowed noticeably and wanted to find an excuse for getting out of this cubicle that made him suddenly feel claustrophobic.

Hector saved him when he said, "That will work, but we have to turn in our reports to our supervisor by eight. Can we meet after then? Say around 8:30?"

"That will suffice, I supposed," Jo answered with reluctance in her voice.

"Fine, then we'll see you two after eight," Hector replied, pulling his partner away from the two women detectives before things really got out of hand.

They both overheard Carol ask her partner, "What was that about, Jo?"

They heard her laugh at Mark's expense when she replied, "He is so adorable! A big old gruff looking man and he is putty in my hands. I knew he was a rookie the moment I laid eyes on him."

"I'd have to admit he was all kinds of flustered with your prick teasing. I wouldn't be a bit surprised that he doesn't complain to his supervisor about you."

"That's the beauty of it Carol," Jo replied before the two agents walked out of earshot. "Joe Armstrong called me while you were talking to Mike from Forensics; he told me to lay it hot and heavy to teach him a lesson. I guess he was messing with him during their first briefing this morning."

"It serves him right then," Carol replied thoughtfully.

The rotten son of bitch, Mark thought to himself.

Hector could not help but laugh at Mark's expense too as they left the building.

"What's so Goddamn funny?"

"Oh, come on Mark," Hector stated with mirth in his voice. "You'd have to admit that was good."

"I don't have to admit to nothing. That was low down and mean of not only her but Joe Armstrong too. I should file harassment charges against both."

"Yeah, well you go right ahead on that one, amigo. I'm sure someone will listen to your tale of woe and feel something akin to pity for you; after they're done laughing at you," Hector replied sheepishly.

Mark did not say another word as they walked quickly to the car and Mark started it up. "Is there anywhere else we need to go?" Mark asked his partner.

"No, I think we did what we were told to do. I guess now we go back to our cubicle and debrief Joe on what we discovered so far. I'm going to ask him to get us a search warrant for the Taj, though."

"Yeah, I'm with you on that one. I need to know what the procedure is on something like that." Mark pulled out the parking space and headed to the Spokane Federal Building. Mark had an idea that he threw at Hector. "How about, after our meeting tonight with those detectives, we go back to the Legion Building to talk with the janitor and security guard?"

"That works for me, Mark. I don't know if we'll get paid for this, though."

"At this point in the investigation, I don't care." Mark found the street he needed and turned down Monroe to Main, where the fleet parking lot was located. Mark saw where Postal vehicles and other Crown Victorias remained parked.

Both agents spotted Joe reading a report from the terminal's monitor as they walked into his office. "Thanks for the little 'got you' I had with that one female detective," Mark said to his boss with sarcasm oozing like honey from his mouth.

"How did you find out?" Joe asked with a wide grin on his lips.

"We overheard her talking about it to her partner," Mark replied non-too-pleased at being the butt of a joke. "Is this a form of hazing or something?"

"Hey, I wouldn't have done that if you had kept your mouth shut and showed me some respect. But instead, you wanted to know about weekends off to see your folks."

"I'm sorry, if I overstepped my bounds here," Mark replied defensively. "Anyway, we're going back to meet them tonight after eight to further debrief them and we thought about going down to the building after ten to talk with the janitor and security guard that found the body. I have a question; when do they pick up the trash?"

"Why ask me?"

"Because the dumpster was empty," Hector stated

"I believe…Hang on I got that in my notes; yeah they pick up early Monday and Thursday mornings. The reason the dumpster was empty when you went there this morning was because the Forensics team took every scrap of trash from the dumpster as evidence," Joe concluded.

Mark and Hector nodded at this bit of logic and continued.

"We contacted a Mr. Brateslav Manovich while we were there. He wouldn't let us inside his business without a search warrant, though," Mark stated making a face of disgust.

"That's fine, Agent Marteau, I'll get that ready for you. What evidence do you have that I can tell the judge, so we can actually obtain this warrant?"

Both men looked at each other as if a bright light had shined on them. "I didn't like the way he looked," Mark replied.

"He did act suspicious, like he had something to hide that he didn't want us to see," Hector continued.

"And he had a foreign accent," Mark concluded.

"I don't believe it," Joe yelled at his men in exasperation. "You want me to make me out to be a laughing stock and embarrass me before a judge over prejudgments? I need evidence that shows him to be a person of interest here! Not that he looks suspicious or he's a foreigner or acted weird."

They both stood at rigid attention, staring straight ahead, not batting an eye as Special Agent Armstrong dressed them down. "Yes Sir!" They replied to their supervisor simultaneously.

"What the hell did you do at Quantico? Sleep while in class?" he asked. "I would have expected this from some numbskull trainee, not two agents with over six months of training!"

"Yes Sir," they both replied together.

"Now go out there and find me evidence that this guy is our man, and I'll be more than happy to get you a search warrant."

"Yes Sir," they replied and did an about-face before heading towards their cubicle. They sat down on their swivel office chairs feeling a heavy weight suddenly descend upon their shoulders as they both slumped forward on their desks.

"Now what do we do?" Mark asked his partner. "I just can't believe no one else talked to this guy before us. Now, he's yelling at us for not showing how clearly guilty he is."

"Let's get busy trying to find evidence, so we can nail this guy," Hector said trying to put an end to this latest fiasco they found themselves "I'm going to do a Google search of his business; find out exactly what he does import and export."

"Where do you suppose he came from?" Mark asked as he went on the internet and typed Inter-Pol in the search bar. He then went to the listing and typed Brateslav Manovich, but nothing came back on that name. *He must be using an alias, but why?*

Hector had slightly better luck as the business came back as a supply chain company. "Look here, boss," Hector pointed out. Mark swiveled his chair to face Hector's monitor and saw Taj Import & Export Company had their main office at 108 South Washington and the warehouse was located at 1501 W. 1st Street, Spokane.

"Who owns this business?" Mark asked.

"Hector scrolled down to the page of Proprietary interest. "It shows Jose Lopez owns the business, along with the names of a number of shareholders, and right here, our friend Brateslav Manovich."

Mark looked closely at the document. "Let's print this up," Mark said. "It's a start. I want to know who this Jose Lopez guy is, plus the rest of these so-called shareholders."

"The problem with that boss," Hector explained to Mark, "I'm seeing that there are addresses all over Mexico and Yugoslavia."

"Well this Brateslav guy lives right here; we saw him ourselves." Mark thought a moment. "We need to check out that warehouse—what goes in and out—that justifies this company's name."

"What are you proposing?"

"Well, if you're game, do a little surveillance tonight on that warehouse, but not traditionally."

Hector looked at Mark with suspicion, "What do you mean 'not traditionally?'"

Mark sighed, "We go there inconspicuously to not create suspicion."

"I'm starting to not like what this is leading to," Hector said with a weary voice.

"Hey, it's why we get paid the big bucks, right?"

"Shit man, I had hoped after talking with that security guard and janitor, we'd go to our hotel room and sleep tonight."

"Well, we still can, Hector. I just want to check it out; an hour at the most," Mark tried to reassure his partner.

"Dude, it's fuckin' cold out there."

"Yeah, and in six months you would complain that it is too hot."

"No, I wouldn't," Hector said quite convincingly.

Mark got up from the swivel chair and went to Joe's office, Hector followed behind. Their supervisor appeared typing in front of a terminal, his back to the door when Mark walked in knocking on the door at the same time. "I found out this Taj Import/Export business has two locations; there's a warehouse on West First that Hector and I want to check out tonight," Mark stated fast, causing Joe to abruptly stop what he was doing and turn around to see what he had to say.

"Hold on a moment, buster," Joe said. "What are you trying to accomplish with this undercover assignment."

"I want to see what this company is importing-exporting; see if it's on the up-and-up."

"Agent Marteau, there are all kinds of companies that call themselves 'import/export.' Yeah you can check it out and report your findings to me tomorrow morning. I don't want you two to go in there half-cocked and create a situation that could get yourselves fired."

"Like I told Hector, it's merely a fact-finding mission, nothing more and it shouldn't take more than an hour," Mark assured Agent Armstrong.

"See that it doesn't; I want a full report on my desk first thing in the morning. Is that clear?"

"Yes Sir," Mark replied snapping his heels to a position of attention.

"Get out of my sight so I can finish writing these reviews."

Mark and Hector went back to their cubicle and continued doing research on the Taj Import & Export Co. "The problem is Mark, on paper it looks one hundred percent legit. Until we dig deeper, we can't do much of anything." Hector pointed out. "I bet though that if we do find anything on them, like you said, it would have to be at that warehouse. I don't think there's anything at that other place we went to earlier."

Mark worried that might be the case, but I will find the underlying cause of this.

Anthony's

Mark and Hector arrived at Anthony's a little after 8:30 and saw the two women sitting at a table near the bar, two half empty drinks sitting in front of them. They seemed immersed in conversation when Mark and Hector came up to their table. They both looked up and smiled with a relaxed air.

"Come and sit down," Jo told the two men. They both scooted back chairs on either side of the two women and sat down obediently. "So, you got your report finished?"

"No," Mark replied pointedly. "We decided when we're done here, to visit the warehouse where Taj Import & Export Company is. We want to see exactly what it is they import or export."

"Really," Jo said with an air of charm and deference, like this was a completely different angle she and Carol had not anticipated in this investigation. "Are you suggesting this is some sort of front?"

"It's possible," Hector said as a server came to their table with an order pad and black pen in hand. "I wish a glass of ice water with a sprig of lime, thank you."

"And you sir?" the tall and thin girl with chestnut colored hair asked Mark.

"I'll have the same," Mark replied.

After she left, Hector continued, "We did a little digging and found Taj is a Limited Licensed Corporation with shareholders of people with less than stellar credentials. The Manovich person we contacted this morning is the son of Nicholas Manovich, head of Yugoslavia Security Agency, which we found out, is equivalent to the CIA and FBI. The Chairman of the board is Jose Lopez, a lawyer for Che Lopez, head of the Todos Santos cartel in Baja California; someone Mark and I are very intimate with."

"How so?" Carol asked, as her attention seemed suddenly riveted to Hector's every word.

"Hector and I took his Nephew back to the United States back in '87, when I was a bounty hunter, for drug smuggling and hiring a pair of assassins to kill a friend of mine.

"He killed Che Lopez' son Carlos in 1977 when I got started informing for the Pasco Police after I witness a friend get killed by Carlos."

"It's starting to sound like you are making a lot of enemies," Carol reasoned as she finished her drink. "Kids, it's been a real pleasure, but I got to get up early and it looks like you two are still on the clock, so have a good night in this wonderful weather," she stated as she got up and placed her coat over her slender body, buttoning up and leaving a dollar tip on the table.

"See you in the morning Carol," Jo said to her partner. She moved a little closer to Mark after she left. "So, what's your next move?"

"After we leave here, we're going to have a talk with the two that discovered the body."

"Oh, that reminds me; the autopsy results came in," Jo stated.

"Anything beyond the pale that we should know about?" Mark asked as he felt her delicate hand brush his knee.

"As a matter of fact, there was. In cases like this, the medical examiner automatically performs a rape kit investigation. There was evidence an attempt was made to sexually assault the girl. There was semen just inside her vagina where the sick son-of-a-bitch tried to penetrate, but got so excited, he ejaculated before breaking through the hymen membrane."

Both men felt intense anger by this news. "That sick bastard," Mark said in a tone suggesting malice towards the person who did this. "Has anyone filed a missing persons' report yet?"

"Not locally, no one has," Jo replied. "I already asked your other two partners in this case to go federal and get Inter-Pol involved too."

"After we talk with the janitor and security guard, we'll look at that import/export place," Mark concluded just as the server arrived with the waters. Both men thanked her, drank down the waters together, slamming the glasses so hard on the table. Jo and the waitress cringed while nearby patrons looked curiously in their direction. "Thanks for inviting us, but we're on the move."

Fort Spokane Brewery

Mark and Hector waited in the Crown Victoria when they saw headlights from two different vehicles pull into the parking lot behind the American Legion Building around eleven that night. They figured to wait a few minutes before going in to talk to them. Suddenly, Mark and Hector saw both men appear from their cars, greet each other, and head down the alley and down Washington Street. "Where the hell are they going?" Mark asked his partner as if he had the answer.

"How the hell should I know? But, I think we need to follow them and find out. One thing I found out while serving in the Marines, people are creatures of habit, even bad habits."

Both men pulled themselves from the four-door sedan and immediately wished they did not have to get out as they felt the cold slap of winter wind across their faces and passing through their coats and hats. They followed the janitor and the security guard at a discreet distance while they walked passed Aunties' Bookstore and further down the street to a pub name Fort Spokane Brewery. They watched the pair walk in and sit down at the bar. Mark and Hector stopped.

"You were right," Mark said. "People are creatures of habit, even bad habits. Based on that, I'm willing to bet those two had no idea when that body was thrown in the dumpster. I would also bet next month's salary that the person who dumped the body in the dumpster probably knew that too."

"What do you want to do?"

"Let's go back to our car and wait for them to get back. I want to know what they really found that night," Mark stated as a simmering anger fueled his psyche.

Two hours later the security guard and janitor made their way, blindly groping for their keys in the dark to let them inside when Mark and Hector got out from their car, slamming the doors hard, startling them.

"Jesus Christ, who is that?" one of the men demanded as they tried to see in the inky darkness.

"FBI," Mark replied in his usual loud baritone voice that seemed to unsettle the two men more. "We need to ask you some questions about the dead girl you found in the dumpster four nights ago."

"Can we go inside first?" the janitor asked. "It's really cold out here."

"I see nothing wrong with that," Hector said good-naturedly. "I get cold easily too; ain't used to this weather you get around here."

The janitor found his set of keys and after many attempts finally found the lock and unlocked the door letting them all inside. The janitor turned on a bank of lights that ran the length of the hallway.

Mark could smell the alcohol on their breaths. "I don't know about you Hector, but I would imagine the company these two gentlemen work for, probably don't have a policy stating you could go off property and indulge in drinking on company time."

"Please, don't say anything," the janitor pleaded. "We're real close to retirement and our wives would kill us if we got fired."

"I don't give a shit," Hector said with frustration. "Why don't you tell that to that girl's parents, who was murdered on your watch?"

Both men stood dumbfounded. The security guard, a medium height and fat man in his early 60s with salt and pepper hair looking disheveled from the stiff breeze blowing outside, responded, "We didn't know nothing about her; just saw the body the next morning before the dumpster showed up. We did everything according to the book."

"But, if you had been here, I would bet you could have seen more than what you're saying and not imbibing in the brew-pub down the street," Mark stated with determination. "Tell us, how long have you been doing this?"

Mark waited for an answer from one of the men, but they did not seem willing to volunteer. "I see we'll need to take you two in for further questioning," Mark finally added.

"No," the short and inconspicuous janitor stated pulling the hat he wore off his baldhead. "We have been doing this for five years now."

"What do you know about Taj Import/Export," Hector asked them.

"I don't know. Sometimes there's someone doing stuff when we come in, but they're usually gone most of the time," the security guard replied.

Mark eyed the janitor, "Does your company contract to clean that office?"

"Yeah, I go in to empty trash and sweep and mop the hardwood floor."

"Have you noticed anything that isn't quite right?"

"I don't know. Sometimes I'm having to pick up a lot of scraps of paper, like the Russian guy was using a shredder."

"On the night you discovered the body, were they still in their office?"

"I don't remember seeing any lights on the sixth-floor window when I drove up," the security guard replied.

"When you discovered the body, besides it being nude, did you notice anything else about her," Mark asked the janitor.

"No, just that she had a heck of a knot on top of her head; was real nasty looking, like she ran into something like a wall," he replied as his hands trembled noticeably.

"Did you discover anyplace where she might have fallen or been pushed into a wall or stairwell?" Hector asked

"Yeah, remember Bob on the third floor, I showed you that mark."

"Yeah, but that could have been anything Bernie," the security guard Bob replied in doubt.

"Show us," Mark commanded.

"Sure, but what do we get out of this?"

Mark looked at Bob in bemusement, before responding, "You don't get to call your wife from Spokane jail asking her to bail your ass out for charges of hindering an investigation." The security guard's mouth dropped but nodded as he led the way through the back hallway to the stairway that led up to the third floor.

Hector asked the janitor on the way up the stairs that were not terribly steep, "Did you clean the spot?"

"Well, yes of course I did," Bernie replied.

"I was afraid of that," Hector said.

"Here is the spot the janitor pointed," Bob said as he stopped at the bottom of the stair landing and noticed the indentation on the wall about four feet off the floor. Mark pulled out a pair of latex gloves and placed them on his bared hands. "Hector, go get the camera."

"You got it Boss," Hector said as he rushed back down stairs to the car where he pulled out a camera, located in the trunk. Hector also spotted the evidence kit and decided to grab that too. The evidence kit was a nylon zippered satchel that had a variety of investigative tools for such a case as this. He ran back up the building where Bob allowed him back inside and they ran up to Mark and Bernie at the fourth-floor landing.

"Great, you brought the evidence bag too," Mark said as he grabbed the camera. "Give me some measurements here, here and here, also measure the distance from the top of the fourth floor to here."

After a time, both men completed their work, writing everything down on their notepads, taking scores of pictures while Hector measured everything. After an hour had passed, they put everything away and left the security guard and janitor there, wondering about their fates. Mark told them as he opened the car door, "I'm not going to mention anything, but I would hope you two, being adults and all, would find the courage to be honest with yourselves, your wives and the company you work for about your obvious drinking problem."

Both men bowed their heads in shame as Mark got inside the cold car and started it up. Hector and Mark left them standing there and Mark commented, "I want to see about finding me a Dodge to drive; I hate Fords."

"Makes no never mind to me," Hector replied. "Are we still going to do the stakeout at the Taj warehouse?"

"Yeah, but like I said, I'm only going there to get a feel—you know a lay of the situation. I think I know what happened; now we need to know why. Based on what Jo told us, I would almost bet she tried to escape and her attacker—the rapist— caught up to the girl and pushed her down the stairs that caused the victim to smack that child's head into that wall, killing her."

"When are you going to let Jo and Carol know?"

"Tomorrow," Mark replied quickly.

Stakeout

Mark and Hector arrived at the warehouse, an old building that appeared vacant, along with most of the buildings on this block. Mark began having second thoughts on this building, but he decided to follow through anyway, hoping that maybe their luck in this case would hold for them. Mark shut off the headlights and parked along 1st Street across from the warehouse. They had an unobscured view of the loading dock locked behind a chain linked fence with three strands of rusted barbed wire stretched loosely on the top, offering a barricade of sorts from unwanted trespassers. He shut off the ignition and waited.

Hector looked briefly at his partner. "I thought we were gonna just check it out, amigo."

"We are," Mark replied tersely. "I want to see if anything goes on. So far, we've been lucky as stuff has just fallen on our laps without us even trying. Bingo; look and check it out."

Coming into view a two-ton panel van, like the one used by moving companies, approached the gate while the passenger, a short, fat man with long hair and bushy beard got out to unlock the entrance and waited for the truck to pass. He immediately closed and locked the access as the driver moved the truck around, its headlights briefly flashing their car, exposing Mark and Hector's surprised expressions.

Nevertheless, apparently, the driver's attention seemed more focused on the side view mirrors as he stopped the van and shifted into reverse. They could hear the warning signal beep out as the truck backed into the loading dock. A beam of light appeared as the garage door slowly rose while the truck slowly backed in and stopped.

Both men heard many voices making demands and then the door closed, slowly muffling the voices until no light or sound emitted anymore. Mark checked the time on his watch and saw it registered 2AM. "Seems to be a little late to be dropping stuff off, don't you think?"

"Not necessarily," Hector replied cautiously. "I would definitely add that to our report that we still have to write." It was a hint that did not go unnoticed on Mark, who yawned noticeably.

"Let's call it a day, my Mexican friend. We'll write out our report, turn it in to Joe, and get our room at the Spokane Club."

The Dream

After they finished their report, Mark and Hector took a room at the Spokane Club. The lobby was spacious, and the concierge seemed very helpful when he learned they were FBI agents. He had white hair and goatee beard, wore wired-rimmed glassed that enhanced his slate gray eyes. He asked, "I know it's none of my business but does your case have anything to do with that girl being found at the Old American Legion Building?"

The question took Mark and Hector back, as they both looked at the older man with a sense of suspicion. Then Mark replied, "Your right, it isn't any of your business."

"That building also used to be the old Spokane Club before they built this one here. It has an interesting history to it, I might add. That's where I got my first job as a bellhop. That's not the first time a murder occurred there, by the way."

Mark and Hector nodded at the old man. They went to their room and went to bed, Hector falling fast to sleep while Mark set the alarm to go off in four hours, just a little after seven and shut off the light.

However, his mind felt overwhelmed from a myriad of thoughts both from the warehouse and from that office at the Old American Legion building. Though his mind and body cried out for much needed sleep, his inner mind kept racing back to the stairway where that indentation on the wall paneling appeared, and whatever industry went on inside that warehouse.

Hector's snoring didn't help Mark to sleep either. He felt as if he was inside a freight train or lying next to a lumberjack using a chainsaw. *I need to know what's inside that warehouse. It cannot be anything legitimate, or there wouldn't be all this secrecy. In addition, where does this girl fit in here? Obviously, she was the victim of an attempted rape, but was she pushed down those stairs because she was trying to escape her rapists? Or, was she killed to keep her quiet and conveniently thrown into the dumpster, like a piece of trash?*

Sometime during the night, maybe fifteen minutes later, Mark's thoughts drifted into REM sleep and his dream took him back to the bottom of the flight of stairs leading to the third floor. He heard a commotion and saw the girl falling forward into the wood paneling and the killer, his face hidden by a mask of shadows, and a strange looking tattoo on his forearm bore numbers and strange lettering like nothing he had ever seen in a language that he wasn't familiar with written around a wheel. He heard her say something but couldn't understand what the language was and then he heard a distant but persistent ding, ding, ding, ding until he awoke and heard the alarm clock buzzing in his ear.

Mark did not mention the dream to Hector; like the dreams he had when he went to face Dave's killers back in '87, they appeared more like visions than dreams, which seemed so real and vivid that Mark felt certain the killer was Brateslav Manovich.

Both men slowly dressed in the same suits they wore the day before when they reported to Joe Armstrong. They did not say a word to each other as their thoughts were more on the case and how best to approach this strategically.

Hector wanted a way inside that warehouse to search everything there that could give them the clues to what it was they figured that the girl knew. Mark wanted to expose Manovich and let the chips fall where they may about whatever the business in the warehouse may entail.

They each grabbed a cup of coffee and Danish on the way out the hotel's lobby where they served complimentary continental breakfast. The cold morning also helped to wake them up as they felt the wind whip up from the Spokane River below the Falls. "Son of a bitch it's cold," Hector complained. "Next time, I'll pick our home base."

Mark laughed at him as they got inside the car and started it up, not waiting to warm it up, Mark backed the car from the parking space and headed around the block back to the Federal building parking lot in the lower level and parked the car. Hector wasted no time as he slammed the door shut and sprinted towards the elevator. Mark followed close behind, though not as quickly.

Undercover

The very moment Mark and Hector walked in, Joe yelled from his office, "Where are those reports you were supposed to have me read first thing in the morning?"

Both men let out a collective sigh as they went to their individual terminals and pulled up the file that showed their reports and they pressed control p on their keyboard. Both reports quickly printed out on the newest technological marvel, the laser jet printer. They quickly ran to the communal printer, pulled their respective reports from the carrousel, then ran to their boss, and handed him their findings and conclusions.

"What time did you get done?" Joe asked.

"We finished the report a little after three," Mark replied quickly.

"I actually finished mine a little before Mark and helped him with punctuation and spelling."

"You did not; you don't know a thing about that shit."

"Why? Because I'm a Mexican?"

"Exactly," Mark replied with a sneer.

"Knock it off you two goof-balls. Go to your desks and give me fifteen minutes to read this before I start making decisions on what to do here." Both men followed Joe's orders as they walked back to their cubicle where they met up with the other half of their team sitting at their desks typing on their terminals. Bob and Howard stopped typing long enough to acknowledge them approaching and then went back to work.

"Gonzales and Marteau, come back here now," they heard their cue from Joe Armstrong yelling for them with an angry voice.

They moved smartly to Joe's office, as they feared they did something terribly wrong. "Yes Sir," both men exclaimed apprehensively.

"Alright, at ease; good job on your first official investigative reports. I see you passed that class okay. Now, based on your recommendations, Mark I am going to hook you up with Bob Smith and interview Brateslav Manovich, here. If he resists in any way, you will use the necessary measures to subdue and apprehend him. Unlike you Agent Marteau, I am not ready to make him a suspect;

more like a person of interest until I read his interview report.

"Agent Gonzales and Agent Jones will work undercover. I want you to go to our Goodwill bin and get the foulest smelling, raggiest looking clothes in there to pass as homeless panhandlers looking for work. Go to Toby's or Mother's to find someone that can get you inside that warehouse. I agree, there is something going on there that appears suspicious, and maybe that girl saw something, or maybe she was part of it from the beginning. Are there any questions?"

"No Sir," they responded smartly as Hector instinctively placed himself back into the position of attention, snapping his heels sharply.

"Standby," Joe ordered. "Agents Jones and Smith, front and center."

They heard a reluctant grumbling come from their cubicle as both veteran agents casually sauntered to Joe's office. "What do you want?" Howard asked his supervisor.

"You two have been together too long and it's time for a shakeup. Jones, you and Gonzales are going undercover to go inside a warehouse at 1501 West First, where you will find out what they're doing in there. Smith and Marteau are going to interview Mister Brateslav Manovich."

"Seriously, Joe?" Howard stated in disbelief.

"Seriously Howard; I'm thinking this can be wrapped up faster with you two veterans mentoring these probies. Plus, I want a little more intimidation where Mr. Manovich is concerned."

An hour later, Mark and Bob arrived back at the Taj Import/Export office at 108 S. Washington on the sixth floor. "Let's take the stairs coming back," Mark suggested. "I wanted to show you and that asshole something; the reason that I'm convinced he is the one and only suspect here."

The elevator opened and both men appeared pleasantly surprised to see Brateslav Manovich standing there, apparently waiting for the elevator.

"Mr. Manovich, you saved us from having to go and knocked on your door," Bob said as he identified himself. "Bob Smith, FBI, and I'm sure you met Mr. Marteau yesterday morning. I understand you demand we show you a warrant to search your office, but we just want to have a friendly conversation with you, and to make it all legal beagle and everything, we'll go to our place at the Federal Building. Nevertheless, to pacify my new partner, we're going to take the stairs. You don't mind, do you?"

"I have no time for this. I go to warehouse. You come back some other day."

"Wrong answer Mr. Manovich," Mark stated as they stood side by side like a pair of linebackers guarding their quarterback, preventing him from passing.

"Please, I already tell you yesterday I did nothing to that little girl."

"Then tell us again at the Federal Building, and if your story checks out, we'll release you to go to your warehouse," Bob stated to the man as they hooked their arms around his two arms and escorted him down the stairs.

"I see that these stairs are neither steep, nor very long," Mark opined as they went down the first two flights of stairs that accounted for maybe half a dozen steps. When they reached the landing going down from the fourth floor down to the third floor though, the stairwell appeared longer and steeper. "I would bet the girl had quite the lead on the man who chased her down the first flights, but he probably caught up to her here, and in his anger at having to chase her in the first place, pushed her hard down the stairs," Mark hypothesized.

"So, I tell you I know nothing about that Bosnian bitch."

Neither man said anything as they escorted him down the stairs. "I'm using that one program that I learned at FBI academy. You know, the one where I write down the numbers of height and weight of the victim, height and weight of the suspect, length of the stairwell and what force it would have taken to produce this," Mark stated as they reached the bottom landing and showed both men the indentation on the wall panel. "You're pretty good size. I'd say about what, one hundred kilos?"

"I weigh one hundred twenty kilos," Brateslav sneered impatiently.

"How much is that, American measure?" Bob asked.

"Around 240 pounds," Mark replied. "How tall are you Mr. Manovich?"

"Two hundred centimeters," he stated with suspicion.

"That's over six feet," Mark affirmed.

"I saw the body of that child," Bob said, "She couldn't have been more than five-foot-tall and doubt if she even weighed 70 pounds. Someone would have been really mad to have picked her up and thrown her down these stairs, for such a nasty looking indentation."

When they went out the back exit, Bob asked Brateslav, "You don't mind if we take our car do you?"

The man said nothing as Mark opened the back door and allowed him inside.

Bob winked at Mark as if saying good job to him as he went to the driver's side, got in, and started the car. "Agent Marteau give that police detective a call and have her and her partner meet us at the Federal Building."

Mark seemed a bit reluctant at first but went ahead and pulled out the detective's business card from his billfold and placed the call on his cell phone. "Jo? Mark here; Oh, I am fine this morning; a little long on the tooth after last night but anyway we are heading to the Federal building with Mr. Manovich. Me and my partner would like to invite you and your partner to the Federal Building to shoot the fat, so to speak with our friend, Brateslav."

Mark listened for a time before responding, "Sure, we'll see you then, Bye."

"She's got a thing for you, Agent Marteau," Bob Smith said with envy in his tone.

"Well, I don't understand it," Mark replied flustered and his face turning beet red.

"You're a man, she's a woman. What is there to understand?"

"I never thought I would be in something like that though," Mark said as he stared out the passenger window watching morning pedestrian traffic on Riverside.

When they arrived at the Federal Building, Mark and Bob escorted Brateslav up to the elevator from the parking garage, and when the door opened on the fifth floor, escorted him to Interview Room Seven. Jo and Carol had just arrived too. Brateslav felt like he would be a part of a tag team match, as his entire attitude changed.

"I demand to see lawyer!" he yelled for all to hear.

Joe Armstrong came running down from his office. "What's going on here?" He demanded upon seeing the two city detectives and his agents with Brateslav Manovich between them.

"I guess he wants to see his lawyer," Bob replied.

"Mr. Manovich, you're not under arrest. We just need to know a few things first," Joe tried to reason with him.

"Why are they here," he demanded pointing at the two women detectives with complete disdain in his expression.

"Well," Bob cut in, "they're here to listen in on your conversation and see if everything you tell us sounds truthful."

"Get lost," Joe told the two women. "That's an order!"

"You can't tell us what to do," Jo stated in frustration and anger.

"Come on Jo," Carol said as she pushed Jo away from the scene. "Joe, you will be hearing from our supervisor about this."

Special Agent Armstrong ignored the threat as he turned to Manovich. "They will be getting a complete transcript of this interview, Mr. Manovich. If you say anything that even remotely sounds untruthful, they will find you and arrest you. I won't stop them either. Am I making myself clear?"

"I don't care about those two bitches. I still demand lawyer."

"You're a defiant asshole, aren't you?" Mark shot back at him.

"That will be enough Agent Marteau. Take him into the interview room and allow him to call his lawyer," Armstrong said to Mark. "You stay outside the door until his lawyer shows up. Bob, come with me."

Mark waited outside while he overheard Manovich talk to someone but in his native language. *A Russian lawyer*, Mark wondered. He heard the conversation at first seemed conversational and short. Then Brateslav began speaking louder as his face became redder and then he became more animated and angry with the person on the other end. He kept hearing "nie, nie" and then a rambling dialogue of the foreign tongue he spoke. He suddenly spat at the phone and disconnected the call. He pulled out his handkerchief from his back pocket and wiped the spittle from the phone.

Mark waited outside the door chuckling as he watched the man stew in his rage.

"FBI agent, come in please," he heard the Serbian man call for him.

Mark turned around and said, "What is it Mr. Manovich?"

"I have problem with my lawyer," he explained through the closed door. "He wants retainer of two thousand dollar before he come down."

"I'm sorry to hear that, Mr. Manovich," Mark replied. "Do you want us to call for a public defender?"

"What is public defender?"

"A lawyer that the court will assign to you if you couldn't afford one," Mark replied. "It's part of your rights in this country," he continued.

"We have same thing in my country; they are notoriously corrupt and mostly worthless."

Mark nodded and watched the man think in the interview room that consisted of three chairs and a bare table. "I will talk to you then, without lawyer."

"So, you wish to waive your right to have an attorney present?"

"Yes, yes; I have nothing to hide."

"Give me a moment then," Mark told him as he left the man and went to get Joe and Bob.

They both appeared engaged in a lively debate over procedure when Mark walked in. "He doesn't want a lawyer now," Mark burst out to the two men. "What do we do?"

"Well, we go ahead and question him, then," Joe replied to Mark as if he was an idiot.

Bob and Mark went back to the interview room, and to both their astonishments, Brateslav disappeared. "Where did he go?"

"I thought the door automatically locked so no one could get out," Mark said with surprise in his voice. Mark looked at Bob for an answer.

"No, you have to manually lock the door with the keys we issued you yesterday morning."

"No keys were ever issued to me, Bob."

"Joe was supposed to issue you and Hector a set of keys."

"Well, he must've forgotten," Mark, replied getting increasingly more frustrated when Joe came up to them.

"What the hell's going on now?"

"Mr. Manovich walked," Mark, replied.

"How? Didn't you lock him in before you left to get your partner?"

"No, because you forgot to issue me keys yesterday," Mark accused his supervisor.

"Son of a bitch," Joe replied. "Okay, here's how this will go, we didn't have enough information from his statement to make an arrest at this time. Is that clear?"

Bob nodded knowingly.

"Sure, but what do we do about Manovich now?" Mark asked.

"See if he shows up again at his office or at the warehouse. If he's not there, then we do know one thing about him."

"What's that," Bob asked.

"He's at least guilty of something."

While Mark and Bob were busy getting Brateslav Manovich, Howard and Hector had dug into the Goodwill bin in the back corner and changed into garb befitting any transient panhandlers. They both wore dark loose-fitting pants with suspenders attached to their belt loops while they found soiled flannel shirts; Hector's had a nasty tear in the elbow and ill-fitting jackets that apparently did little to keep out the winter chill. Both wore boots that appeared much too big for them.

They dressed in their dressing area and snuck out back behind the Federal Building's garage where they slowly moved their way through downtown until they came upon Toby's on Second just passed Washington.

Howard walked up to the bar while Hector found a table near the entry. The place appeared deserted save for the ancient looking woman bartender, who might have been a hooker in her early days, though neither man could be certain what her age was.

"What can I do for you boys," the woman asked with a bit of a harsh cackle in her throat that sounded like she needed to spit out a large mass of phlegm.

"You want a beer there, friend?" Howard asked Hector. Hector waved him off purposefully evading any eye contact, as if he was an outlaw wanted for some grisly crime.

"I'll take a shot of that whiskey you got there," he pointed at the fifth of half full Monarch bourbon.

"That would be a buck a shot," she said to him as she eyed him with suspicion.

"I see. By the bye, you don't know of any work around here a man could get, you know under the table?" Howard asked as he pulled out a wadded-up piece of paper and handed it to her.

"What the hell is this?"

"An IOU," Howard said innocently.

"I don't take IOUs, just cash. Now pay me a buck for your shot or get the hell out of here."

"Okay, okay, here you go. Here's a fiver for you," Howard said as he gave a crumpled-up bill with Lincoln's likeness on the face to her.

She glared at him as she went to the cash register and handed him back his change. "There's a warehouse over off First and Cedar. It doesn't pay good, but people like you and your friend would probably fit right in," she informed him.

"Is there someone there that we could talk to?"

"He calls himself Ivan, though I don't really know if that's his real name. He's plenty big and real scary looking too, and he has a thick Russian accent. He comes here around four every day and again when I open at six in the morning. He's always hiring; I guess if you got a driver's license you get more."

"Thank you honey, you've been very charitable to us. Here is a tip for your trouble. My friend and I will be here this afternoon. Have a good day madam. Come along my bashful friend; let's find a shelter to sleep at until 4 o'clock."

A little after 4 o'clock in the afternoon, Hector and Howard walked into Toby's, their jackets zipped to their necks and collars pulled up around their ears. Sitting with his back to the far wall, at a booth, surrounded by a group of four big white men with clean-shaven heads, was the man everyone called Ivan. Hector immediately recognized him as Brateslav Manovich. He held back behind Howard, again purposefully evading eye contact with everyone.

Howard went up to the group but acted nonplus at the much larger men. "Good evening gentlemen, I was told by the lovely bartender this morning a certain fellow named Ivan may be looking to hire day laborers who need some money to get a hotel for a week's let. Is Ivan about?"

"I am Ivan," the man in the middle of the group said with a thick Eastern European accent that Howard immediately recognized as Serbian.

"Da li govori srpski," Howard asked.

"Ja da," the big man affirmed in Serbian.

"I'm sorry, but that is all the Serbian I know. Allow me to introduce myself; I am Theodore Rutherford Washington, and this is my dear deaf-mute friend Jesus Gomez, we came in on a train from the south. We need some work to afford food and lodging."

"Do you have license to drive truck?" Ivan asked the hobo directly, but his gaze fell upon the short Mexican in the back as someone that looked familiar.

"My good man, I most certainly can drive a truck, but unfortunately our wonderful justice system found it fitting to take my license some time ago for a couple of minor traffic violations. But, I assure you, I will drive with the utmost discretion."

"Fine, fine. How do I talk to deaf mute friend?" He got up from the table and stood in front of

Hector trying really hard to remember where he had seen him before.

"I use lip reading and sign language," Howard replied. "Observe; Jesus, we might be working for this man. His name is Ivan." Howard talked at him as if he was a half-wit, purposefully slow, pointing at Ivan and doing any number of hand gestures and talking so loud people across the street could hear him.

"AHH, AHH," Hector replied as if a cat had cut his tongue out. "A gow maw caod?"

"Yes, yes exactly. He will pay us cash," Howard replied.

"You report at 11:30 tonight and no drinking," Ivan stated evenly, still looking at the Mexican looking man with a certain curiosity. "I still don't know about deaf mute one. How can I communicate with him? I do not know this sign language you used."

"I assure you that he read lips quite well."

"But, we don't always speak English; sometimes we speak Serbian.

"That's quite alright, he only understands Spanish; sometimes he might understand English."

"Oh, okay I hire him then. You be at warehouse 11:30 sharp!" he yelled at Hector, pronouncing each word slowly and loud as well.

Hector smiled at the man they call Ivan and nodded like an imbecile. "Goed naw mak too."

"What did he say?"

"God bless you," Howard replied. "Could you see it in your heart to give us a small meal to hold us over?"

"Nerman, give them each two dollar for meal," Ivan ordered as a burly man half again as big as Ivan came forward.

He pulled out a large wad of bills and flipped through until he came down to the one-dollar-bills and handed each man two dollars. "Now go and be there at warehouse by 11:30."

Hector and Howard left Toby's and went toward the Zips Drive Inn. Each ordered a burger and fries. Howard kept looking outside, ensuring that they were being followed. Sure enough, they only had to wait three minutes before one of Brateslav's goons strolled by and looked inside the window. Howard waved at him as they waited for their order to be filled. The man scowled at them, did an about-face and walked back to Toby's.

"Do you think they suspected us," Hector asked Howard between bites of the burger.

"I don't know; he sure was looking at you a lot though. Do you know why?"

"It's because his name isn't Ivan, it's Brateslav Manovich and we met yesterday. It's a good thing you mentioned I was a deaf mute, or my voice more than likely would have given me away, and our cover would have been blown."

"It may already have," Howard replied as concern fell like rain from his voice.

"It's all good. I think you being the driver will probably be the key here anyway. They'll probably just want me unloading that crap, or whatever they'll have us do," Hector continued.

"I hope you are right on this. Give us another ten minutes and then we will walk to the Otis Hotel. Our room is 201. I'll call Joe from there letting him know what the game plan is so far."

"Sounds like this isn't your first undercover assignment," Hector asked in the form of a statement more than a question.

"It's not," Howard replied. "My and Bob's first case together was an undercover assignment concerning a kidnapping that happened in Idaho and found the perps here waiting for the ransom to exchange hands. Unfortunately, the victim was never found, and the suspects got away."

"They're probably still in Idaho," Hector said between bites of fries.

"Yeah, well rather than try to go out and find them, Joe had us sweep it under the rug, as if it didn't happen, so there would be no blame game to go around."

"Are you serious?"

"That's how things are done, at least where Joe is concerned. He'll leave a cold case cold to protect his ass, rather than do something that might get him fired."

"Unfuckingbelievable," Hector whispered.

After ten minutes, they went to the Otis Hotel, which was nothing more than a slum occupied by the down and out, the hookers and the drug addicts who couldn't get into anything else. Room 201 came upon them off the left as they walked to the door and Howard unlocked it. Inside was a myriad of electronic surveillance equipment, binoculars on a tripod and other items that could be used to eavesdrop on a potential suspect.

"We have similar rooms at the Ridpath, The Red Lion and the Carlyle," Howard told Hector in hushed tones.

Hector nodded at Howard, a bit impressed by what he was exposed to. Howard went immediately to a phone and dialed a number. After a moment, Hector heard Howard say "Dwarf." "211649009," he replied. "Bobcat," he answered and waited. "Joe, this is Howard, we're in. Yeah, we report at 11:30 and I'm apparently driving. One thing, Hector and the guy met yesterday; he's Brateslav, but everyone at Toby's called him Ivan. No, I think I saved the day when I told them he was a deaf mute. Howard hung up and said, "Good luck, Joe told me to tell you. He wants you to find anything, bills of lading, and receipts, whatever that appears like this stuff is being hijacked and repackaged and sent to other places."

"I had that in mind to do anyway," Hector stated. He watched Howard going to camera boxes and gathering film. "What are you doing?"

"I need a camera to take pictures. I have a feeling, these guys, if they are doing what I think they are doing, don't play nice and chances are they rarely leave witnesses or evidence behind."

"Oh okay, so you're going to try and get pictures to incriminate them?"

"That's the plan," Howard replied.

"That makes no sense, man. If we're undercover, how are you gonna get away with taking pictures of this?"

Howard thought a moment, and realized Hector was using common sense and he was right, the logic of a homeless man pulling out a very expensive camera and taking pictures did not make sense. He put the camera back. He sighed and said, "It looks like you will have to be the hero tonight."

"Agents Marteau and Smith get your asses up here," Joe Armstrong yelled after talking to Howard on the secured line from the Otis Hotel. They both came to his office, Mark a little quicker than Bob, who seemed to always pull up the rear.

"What's going on?" Mark asked his supervisor.

"You and Bob are off the hook. Brateslav was found." Both men sighed. "He apparently goes by the alias of Ivan and hires drifters and homeless men to do day labor. Howard and Hector were hired for work tonight and Howard is driving a truck. At this point, we don't know what this job will be, but I'm thinking that he should have a guardian angel watching over him."

Mark watched Bob nod when he asked, "Is Hector going on this too?"

"I couldn't say, but he immediately recognized Mr. Manovich, and he has suspicions about Hector, like he's seen that face before, but can't quite place it. Howard's quick thinking placed Hector as a deaf mute and they just came off the train, which could mean anywhere."

"Hector is anything but a mute," Mark laughed at this. "But, if he can pull it off, more power to him."

"I want you two to follow the van after 11:30 and see where it goes," Joe told his team.

"Are you certain there is only one van?" Bob asked with skepticism in his voice.

"I can answer that," Mark said. "When we were there last night we only saw one van back into the loading dock at around 1:30. If what they are doing is hijacking other semis, then it must be reasonably close, perhaps no further than the Idaho Panhandle."

"Good observation, Marteau. Follow them at a reasonable distance. If the driver is Howard, I told him to tap his brakes four times, and that you would flash your high beams once, so that he would know." Joe started to look concerned when he stated, "At no time are you to engage this, unless Howard's life is endangered. Even if it means witnessing them killing the semi driver," Joe continued.

"Shit, it sounds like some real serious stuff going on," Mark said in astonishment.

"I've dealt with similar cases before, and believe me; it's never pretty or clean." Joe looked at his team. "Take off to get yourselves rested and be at that warehouse by 11:45 at the latest; any questions?"

"Before you called us back here, I entered the data I got from the third-floor landing where we found that indentation. I suspected that girl was pushed. Based on everything, including the height and weight of Mr. Manovich, who graciously volunteered that information this morning while we were bringing him in. He also told us she was Bosnian.

"Anyway, I just got the results and Mr. Manovich is the most likely suspect to have pushed that girl and produce that much momentum to cause the indentation on that panel. By the way, has anyone from the Bosnian community come forward to place a missing person's report?"

"Not to my knowledge. Tomorrow I will place a request to the judge for a search warrant for that office and the warehouse. Anything else?" Joe asked.

Neither man said anything. "Very well then," Joe continued. I will be monitoring everything from the Ridpath. Use tach channel three on your radio. Remember, this is only a surveillance mission tonight. When we get the evidence, we need to bust them, then we will go in armed and ready." He looked directly in their eyes and said, "Good Luck."

Howard and Hector arrived at the warehouse on West First. It was a little after 11:25 as Howard knocked on the Entry door on Railroad Street. The sign over the façade had long ago faded and Hector could barely make out "Rodger's Motors and Engine Repair." Someone on the other side cracked the door and the person looked at them briefly and asked, "Who sent you?"

"Ivan," Howard replied in a whispered voice.

The man motioned both inside as he quickly closed and locked the door. "They aren't here yet," a tall, wiry man said as his eyes darted from Howard to Hector and back to Howard. "Did Ivan tell you anything about the load?" he asked in an overly anxious voice that raised alarm bells in both men.

"Why no my good friend," Howard replied. "He just mentioned to me about needing a driver and my companion here will help with loading or unloading. My name is Theodore Rutherford Washington, and you might be?"

"I'm Nick, okay—no last names, though. It's better that way. Who are you," he asked Hector who stood there motionless.

"His name is Jesus," Howard stated for him. "He was born without the benefit of hearing or speech; he can read lips, but only in Spanish and sign language."

"How the hell are we going to talk to him then? I don't know any Spanish except like, you know, 'si' or 'adios.'"

"Ahhh, Ahhh," Hector blurted out with a smile, as if he understood for the first time and smiled at Nick, slapping him on the shoulder.

"There you go," Howard said with enthusiasm. "Whenever you want him to do something just tell him 'si or adios,' and he'll do it."

Both men looked around them for the first time and saw furniture and household electronics, like televisions and stereos, wrapped tightly in cellophane, loaded on pallets. "So, are we in the moving business?" Howard asked Nick.

"Don't ask any questions!" He demanded in a harsh whisper. "Is that clear?"

"Of course, my friend," Howard replied with an edge of concern in his voice.

Just then, a horn sounded outside as Nick ran over to the chain and pulled the overhead door up. As the door steadily opened, the rear of a two-ton van appeared. "Si, Si," Nick yelled at Hector who was looking at the van, pretending not to hear him yelling.

Howard tapped Hector on the shoulder, pointed at Nick, and then twisted his hands in a multitude of directions that would make any deaf person confused and angry. However, Hector nodded enthusiastically as he went to the van and raised the door. Inside, the cargo hold was empty. Brateslav and Nerman appeared as they threw in a mover's dolly, some duct tape and rope inside.

"Adios, adios," Nick told Hector.

"Why you say that to him? He don't go nowhere," Brateslav said to Nick with confusion in his voice.

"Those are the only Spanish words I know that he understands," Nick replied.

"You are idiot. You told him goodbye."

"Well, I don't know what thank you is in Spanish," Nick said defensively.

"Gracias is word for thank you. You are such an idiot. Igor, where is my car?"

"In front, gazda," a thick neck man with massive head and arms that looked even more massive said to Brateslav.

"You, Theodore, I want you to drive and Nerman will be navigator. Do nothing but drive and do not help in any way. You tell deaf mute friend he will work here with Nick to get space ready for new stuff. Three more people come, and they help too. We be back no more than three hours, then everyone helps unload truck. Let's go."

He tapped Hector on the shoulder and said to Jesus while moving his hands about as if he was drying them on a hand towel, "You must stay here and help Nick my friend. I'll be back soon. Goodbye."

After they got in their vehicles and took off, Hector helped Nick move pallets about to create space for the next load about to come in. Nick used a pallet jack while Hector moved loose boxes and placed them on pallets too.

While he wasn't looking in his direction, Hector discreetly pulled bills of lading from boxes and placed them in his pockets. He never really checked beyond the destination the package was supposed to go. However, it appeared apparent they were not destined for here, as most had towns like Missoula, Billings and Fargo written in bold letters with barcodes appearing next to the destination. Hector wanted to know more about this when he heard the rollers of the pallet jack move over the concrete floor. He quickly stuffed everything inside his light coat jacket.

He heard Nick yelling "si, si," at him, which he ignored, and then just happened to look up. He smiled like a fool while Nick beckoned him over with long, sinewy arms. Hector went over to Nick as he showed him more boxes to pack on a pallet that he set down on the floor. He noticed the bills of lading on these boxes showed Salt Lake City and Cheyenne. "Si, si," Nick told him as he gyrated his arms and hands in a spasm of motions. Hector nodded excitedly, as he picked up the boxes and pulled the bills of lading.

"No, don't do that," Nick admonished, forgetting his companion was deaf. Hector, for his part, looked confused and stated, "Ah gowl mo."

"I don't know what you said," Nick replied. He saw Hector look at him as if he was a living, breathing question mark. "Adios."

"Ahhh," Hector replied and proceeded to pull the bills of lading from the boxes as he packed them on the pallet.

"Son of a bitch," Nick stated throwing up his arms in a sign of defeat as he went about helping to finish placing the boxes on the pallet; then the phone rang. Hector heard the phone's ringing, loud and obnoxious, but acted like nothing happened as he saw Nick run up to the office on a second story and answer the phone. Hector listened to the one-way conversation and then Nick abruptly hung up. As near as Hector could gather, the help was either here or on their way. A horn sounded, and Nick had to run to the overhead door and began raising it.

A black panel van had backed to the loading dock and three men climbed up from the van pulling with them three young girls. They seemed to range in age from twelve to sixteen as Hector noticed this while still placing the remaining boxes on the pallet. "Who is that?" one of the men asked in a heavily accented Eastern European dialect.

"It's okay, he's deaf and dumb. He's harmless," Nick stated. "I hope these girls are better than the last one you brought. She was useless, and we had to get rid of her."

"Are you sure he deaf?"

Nick appeared to get angry with the man and yelled at Hector, "Hey you over there." Hector for his part, ignored Nick as he went to a deck broom and began sweeping the floor. He could hear one of the men pulled his handgun from his holster with the intent to fire the gun inside the building. "Hey man, not inside the building," Nick told the man.

"I want to make good he deaf," the Eastern European man replied.

"By shooting your gun inside the building? Ivan would have your head," Nick reiterated. "You better move your van before they get back; it's almost time."

Nick watched one of the men jump off the loading dock, get into the van and start it up, pulling the van out to the side of the building. "Where are they from?" Nick asked the two remaining men.

"They are all sisters from Croatia. They will make good wives, or sex toys," the man replied with a sneer and a smile born of pure evil. Hector saw he looked overweight, with long black hair and heavy black beard that covered this chest.

Hector then used his peripheral vision to see what the three young girls looked like. They shivered, perhaps because of the cold—they had on very thin cotton dresses with shoes, but no socks and light sweaters buttoned as far as it would reach. Or, perhaps because they feared for their lives being surrounded by these strange men. They had long and straight black hair with bushy eyebrows and a slight brown tint to their skin. Their noses appeared long and straight and their lips looked tight and pursed, probably to keep their teeth from chattering.

They noticed the big van backing up and when it stopped, the heavy set, bearded one raised the van's cargo door as Brateslav pushed a bloodied Howard inside. "What is this?" he asked in their native tongue.

Hector, for his part, knew the timing was all wrong. *They're here way too early*, he thought as he saw the frightened girls and placed his finger to his lips and slipped away while all four laborers had their attention averted.

"He is informant for FBI. Find deaf mute asshole and kill them!" Brateslav screamed in Serbian as he pushed Howard to the cement floor.

Earlier Hector noticed another door most likely used as a fire exit and ran to it, opening the door and going out that way. He heard Brateslav screaming as he softly closed the door behind him.

The door put him on Cedar Street and remembering the Otis Hotel was just a couple blocks east., Hector ran around the block onto First and up the street. He saw no traffic, though a local dive bar remained open with a couple of drunks sitting inside and the bartender, a middle-aged man with balding head, yelling at them to finish up and get out. Hector ran as hard as he had ever run his entire life. Hector heard gun fire erupted and he sprinted to the lobby.

He just went into the front entry of the hotel where its lobby looked as ram shackled and run down as the façade, when he spotted the large sedan speed past.

Perhaps it was them. But, Hector felt he could not take any chances, as he slipped inside Carriage House, a run-downed restaurant where bus passengers went to grab a quick meal before leaving Spokane; or the first impression that visitors received once they arrived. Hector watched the car go down the street. *Either he didn't see me, or he just did not think I am worth the hassle,* Hector thought. He then ran up to the stairs to the second floor and reached 201, to the locked and dead bolted door. Hector did not have the key.

Discovered

Howard pulled the cumbersome two-ton van out onto First, turning quickly onto Cedar and then to Sprague Avenue that meandered onto Maple and Pacific, before hitting one-way traffic of Maple.

He maneuvered the van pass a maze of one-way streets that appeared to be an Achilles heel to someone unfamiliar with downtown Spokane. But, Howard negotiated expertly to the East I-90 to Coeur d-Alene on ramp sign and moved slowly up to freeway traffic. Traffic this time of night appeared mostly sparse with more truckers on the freeway than cars. It took no time for the van to merge into traffic, though it took a bit longer for Howard to shift the van into highway cruising speed.

Howard heard Nerman talking with Brateslav on the CB radio as he saw a black Mercedes jet passed them going well pass 75 miles per hour on the inside lane. Howard saw another pair of lights steadily approaching, he could tell they were the familiar Crown Victoria headlights the FBI had, and he gently tapped the brakes four times when he saw the car flashed its high beams once, ensuring that Howard had his back up, if he needed them.

Just before the Barker Road exit, Nerman told Howard, "You get off here."

"Very well my friend," Howard stated, remaining in character. *It is too soon, Howard thought. Have they found me out? How?*

He saw the big black Mercedes parked on the side of the road, its hazard lights flashing in the early morning darkness. *Why are they stopping here? Did they experience car trouble?*

"You stop here," Nerman ordered as he saw Brateslav get out from his car.

"Get out, Theodore. Let me talk," Brateslav told his driver. Howard followed orders and a sense of fear formed in the pit of his stomach as he jumped down from the truck to face the two hundred fifty-pound man. "You are so very clever Theodore, and you must think us Serbians are all so stupid."

"I don't understand, Ivan."

"Oh, but I think you do." Cars passed by them and he grabbed Howard and lifted him up with no effort pushing him hard against the side of the moving van and punching him hard in the face and again in the gut. "Who are you, really? FBI?

I knew it," Brateslav yelled in satisfaction. "I knew you are FBI informant. Open back door. Nerman, you drive back to warehouse. It will be easy to clean up mess there than here; no witnesses either, except for deaf mute Mexican. We kill him too anyway."

How did they know? Howard asked himself.

"Nerman told me, you drove through Spokane like an expert, yet you claim this afternoon you just came here off train from somewhere south of here," Brateslav replied to the unspoken question as if he could read Howard's mind. Brateslav then ungraciously threw him into the empty cargo bay of the truck as he hoisted himself inside after him and closed the overhead door.

Raid

Mark and Bob were about to leave for the warehouse when Mark's cell phone rang, and he answered it, "This is Agent Marteau, FBI."

"Yeah, this is the janitor over at the Old American Legion Building. I think I found something that might interest you. Can you come down ASAP?"

"Sure, we'll be right down there," Mark replied. "Bob, we need to take a quick detour to the American Legion Building. That janitor thinks we found something."

Bob quickly checked his watch and saw it was closing in on mid-night and he felt nervous about leaving his partner in a situation he might not be able to get out of. "Okay, but we have to make this quick. Are you clear on this Agent Marteau?"

"Of course," Mark replied as they went to the car and started it up. They drove up to the Legion Building ten minutes later and found the janitor waiting patiently outside near the dumpster.

Mark went up to Bernie and exchanged handshakes before he asked, "What have you got?"

Bernie shivered as he opened the dumpster and using his latex gloved hands retrieved a trash liner filled with shredded documents and other pieces of paper that Mark and Bob guessed to be receipts. "I didn't dump that neither. It had to have been that Russian. I bet he must be getting ready to skedaddle."

Mark nodded as he donned his own latex glove and pulled the filled bag from the dumpster and placed it into the back seat of the Crown Victoria. He immediately fished out Jo's card and called her cell number.

"Sorry to wake you Jo, but we found some stuff that might be our break in the case. Can you meet us at your office in five minutes?"

"Shit Mark, you picked a fine time to call me. I was about ready to turn on my vibrator and get a good night's sleep."

"Oh, well I'm really sorry, Jo," Mark stammered as he felt his face redden and it suddenly felt very hot out here in this zero-degree parking lot.

"Relax Mark; I'm still here at the office, just finishing up on a report. Come on down." She disconnected the call and Mark closed the phone looking dubious and embarrassed.

"Here's the thing, Agent Marteau; sure, we can drop that shit off and it most likely has damaging evidence, but just remember Howard's life is on the line here, and it will be on your conscience if something bad happens."

"I understand, but this may be the break we need to put his ass away forever. I just want to give her the bag of trash, so she can go through it and see what's inside."

Bob sighed heavily, then he reluctantly nodded saying, "Okay, let's go get this done. I'll drive though; I know a short cut to get there."

"That works for me," Mark replied. "I just got lucky to have found it at all yesterday."

In five minutes, Mark handed the shredded documents to Jo who looked completely frustrated that he would task her to decipher this while he took off to do surveillance somewhere.

"I want you back here as soon as you're done so you can help me," she barked at his back as he headed quickly out the door.

Mark checked the time on his watch, ran to the Crown Victoria, and heard Bob muttering under his breath, "If he gets killed, you tell his wife and kid all about it."

"I understand," Mark replied as he felt the g forces press against his stomach when Bob gunned the car down Broadway to Monroe and across the bridge. Bob took a right onto second with the intent of taking a right on Jefferson when Mark saw the van moving down Maple. "There it is," Mark told Bob as he spotted the van. Bob sped up, took an immediate left onto Maple, and saw the Mercedes Benz tailing the van as it drove up the onramp to the freeway.

Bob immediately held back as they followed and waited to see what the Mercedes was going to do next. "I'm pretty certain that Black car is part of the team. Let's see what he does," Bob said as they went up the on ramp and saw the black sedan pass the van.

"Just as I thought," Bob said. "The Mercedes will be tagging the truck, another vehicle, possibly a big truck or SUV will do something to make their target semi pull over—perhaps shoot out his tires—they go down and force the driver out and either kill the driver right there or make him drive to a secluded location.

"Okay, Howard has tapped his brakes, now let's just go along for the ride and see what happens. Go ahead and call Joe to let him know everything is a go."

"You got it," Mark replied as they kept a steady distance. He called Joe on the portable radio. "Joe, you got a copy?"

"Roger," Joe replied.

"Everything is a go."

"Roger, out," Joe said.

"And that's it until we see the action. Then I want you to be in constant communication with

Joe. He's the boss, so we'll do exactly what he tells us. Is that clear Marteau?"

"Yeah, I heard you," Mark said in a tone of grudging acceptance.

When they took the Barker Road exit, Bob showed concern. "Why are they going there?" Bob asked himself aloud.

Mark didn't say anything but held the radio to his mouth as Bob shut off the head lights and pulled to a stop as the Crown Victoria idled in the freezing night. "Joe, we might have a possible situation, over," Mark stated into the radio.

"Sitrep," Joe ordered.

"Truck pulled off highway at Barker Road."

"Copy, is there a hijacking in progress?"

"Negative; have no hijacking; Partner is using night vision scope to see what the situation is."

"Tell Joe that Howard is out of the truck. Oh shit, I think he's been found out."

"Howard has been compromised, repeat, Howard has been compromised," Mark stated trying to sound as professional as possible, though he felt his own emotion trying to get the best of him.

"Roger, go passed parked vehicles so that they think there is traffic and they won't try to take him out. Wait for them to leave and follow them."

"Roger," Mark replied. Bob put the car in gear, turned on the headlights, and drove past the truck just as both saw Brateslav throw Howard against the truck's side. Mark so wished he could get out and take care of them but realized too they had a bigger catch to make. Bob drove about one hundred yards past and pulled the car over. Once again, he turned off the lights and waited. A moment later, they observed the Mercedes and truck make a "Y" turn and head back to the overpass and back to I-90 returning to Spokane.

After another five minutes, Bob maneuvered the Crown Victoria around and followed. "I bet my month's wages they're taking him back to that warehouse," Bob stated. Mark nodded as he went on the radio.

"Joe, latest sitrep," Mark said

"Roger, go ahead with sitrep."

"Van and black Mercedes heading west on I-90, possibly heading to warehouse," Mark replied.

"Good copy; proceed to warehouse and wait for me and local law enforcement backup."

"Roger, will do," Mark said as he felt a building tension in his body and an urge to puke. *What's wrong with me? I didn't act like this before at Todos Santos or in Pennsylvania.* Everything around him appeared so surreal at this moment as Bob picked up the pace and passed both vehicles and Mark noticed the speedometer needle striking past eighty miles per hour.

They reached the warehouse just as they noticed a van pull up and witnessed three teenaged girls being pulled inside by three men. Mark's cellphone rang on him as he answered, "Hello?"

"This is Jo, we have enough from these shredded documents to put this man in prison for a very long time. Not only was he running a racketeering oper-ation, where he hijacked semis and stole their loads, he was also running some sort of sex slave racket. I haven't found anything on the Jane Doe though."

"Thanks. Can you come down to the ware-house and bring some uniforms with you?"

"The one you were talking about earlier at 1501 W. First?"

"Yeah, that's the place," Mark replied.

"We'll be right there; wait, a dispatch call just now went out. I'll be there in no time. Bye."

Mark disconnected and placed the phone back inside the pocket of his coat. "That was Jo, the female detective…"

"Yeah, I sort of overheard the conversation. All right, I want you to be very careful and don't be stupid by playing hero to impress her. She is a professional and knows how to handle herself quite well. Do I make myself clear?"

"Yes, you do," Mark replied.

"I don't know what your past is and all I know is that you are a probie—a rookie with not a whit of experience in this sort of situation. If you prove me wrong, so be it, but for the sake of argument and my own peace of mind, just do what me and Joe tell you."

"Point taken, Bob," Mark said. "At another time, when the opportunity presents itself, I'll tell you all about my experiences."

"Fair enough. Here they come; get yourself ready."

Mark pulled out the service pistol, a Glock Model 22 .40 S&W.

"You got the Glock? I still have the Colt .45," Bob stated enviously.

Mark smiled at that when they saw Joe's car approach from across the old library. A small pin light flashed three times at them and Bob did the same with his pin light. All three men got out from their cars while three additional units from Spokane Police converged. They all went to the warehouse just as the moving van backed up to the loading dock and they saw the big Serbian driver get out from the truck.

Mark pounced on him first, throwing his forearm into his face, staggering him briefly when he went for his gun, but discovered almost too late police had him surrounded and he surrendered immediately. The same situation occurred between another officer and the Mercedes driver as both men were escorted to a waiting patrol car.

All three went inside, followed by six uniformed officers and Jo, who Mark just barely caught sight of prior to going inside the warehouse.

Joe screamed, "Federal Bureau of Investigation, freeze where you are. You're all under arrest."

Brateslav pushed Howard at Agent Armstrong and ran outside, pursued by three officers and Bob. Mark heard shots fired. He then saw another one of Brateslav's henchmen pull out his sidearm and fire at a couple officers. Mark returned fire, dropping the man to the floor, a round squarely in his chest. He stopped breathing.

Nick immediately surrendered, whimpering as two officers took him down and placed cuffs over his wrists.

Mark looked about the warehouse and caught sight of Jo as she talked briefly to a uniformed sergeant. Where is Hector?

"Hector, where are you?" Mark yelled out to his partner and friend.

"Who are you yelling for? The only other person here is that deaf mute named Jesus," Nick called out over his shoulder as the officers led him out the side door of the warehouse.

It occurred to Mark that Hector, upon realizing their cover was blown, must have left. He went over to Howard sitting on a chair, being looked over by Joe, when he asked, "Was there a place that Hector could have gone?"

Howard looked at Mark as if he was an idiot when he said, "He's at the Otis Hotel, more than likely. It's just up the street from here."

Just then, Bob came in and announced, "That bastard got away!"

"Like I told you two earlier, he's guilty of something," Joe Armstrong stated. "Go to the airport and I'm sure you'll find him trying to buy a ticket out of here."

"How about Hector?" Mark asked.

"Howard and I will rescue him. Don't just stand there waiting for an invitation, go!"

Mark and Bob left the warehouse and drove to the airport. When they arrived, they went up and down all four concourses, but didn't see any sign of him.

"Do you think Joe got it wrong? That he went to the bus depot or the train station?" Mark asked Bob as a feeling of frustration threatened to overwhelm him.

Otis Hotel

Joe and Howard drove to the front of the Otis Hotel twenty minutes later as they went up the second floor to room 201 but did not see Hector.

"Behind you," Hector announced to the two agents. "What the hell took you so long? I was freezing my ass off up here."

"We were held up in traffic," Howard replied nursing a nasty looking bump on his head, but no worse for wear.

"Did we get our man?" Hector asked Joe.

"We got his operation," Joe replied. "And they all seem extremely willing to talk. Bob and Mark are at the airport looking for Brateslav Manovich." Joe's cell suddenly chimed, and he answered the phone. "Really? Son of a bitch that really sucks. Are you sure he's nowhere in that airport? He had to have gone somewhere. Okay, I will put out an APB for all airports, bus and train stations. I can't believe he got away like that," Joe told Bob and Mark on the other end.

Hector's Call to Duty

October 15, 2014

Hector's nap was at best half-ass. Every time he attempted to doze off, some other memory, that memory that haunted him to this day, materialized. He realized what Mark wanted from him earlier.

He wants a confession about what I know. He wants me to retell that time, that awful day, Hector said to himself. *I promised Joe I wouldn't say anything about what happened that day. Should I break that promise to give my best friend a sense of closure? Though, by doing that very thing could mean he would hate me forever? Now is not the time, Mark.*

Before leaving for Mark's place, Agent Brodzinski handed him the folder, but it wasn't from the FBI's archives, but a translated version sent to her from Ismet Princip, newly appointed head of Serbian Information Agency. Included in the folder, was the same letter he read in Joe Armstrong's office from Che Lopez fourteen years ago.

August 24, 2000

The day that Joe sent Mark down to San Juan, as a favor for his friend, and former FBI agent, Captain Rodrigues, he called Hector back to his office. Hector noted that on this late August afternoon he had hoped to be going on a well-deserved vacation soon. Much to his dismay, that would not be happening this year at least.

Hector walked into Joe's new office, after his promotion to station chief. Hector saw the Spokane skyline from Joe's office window. He looked down at the man who he considered a toady and quite lazy. "Hey Joe, did you call me in?"

"Yes, I did. Come on in and sit down." Joe still had handsome, leading man looks and he knew it, though his eyes had begun to darken, and his trimmed brown hair had begun to recede around the edges. "The reason I called you in is because NSA intercepted this email from Che Lopez to one Nicholas Manovich, head of Serbian Security Service, a government agency more like our CIA than FBI. Part of their trade is political assassinations.

"In this case, though, it appears to be Mark's parents, one Nicole Baker, and her son Dylan are the marks. When I dug back to when Mark filled out his security background paperwork, there was never any mention of Ms. Baker or Dylan Baker, yet, according to this letter, it appears they are very close friends; been so for quite some time now.

"I have the translated version of the letter for you to read. It doesn't take a rocket scientist to figure out these four people are in grave danger and need our help to protect them from potential assassination attempts. I need you to go down there and find out all you can, plus try your damnest to protect these four individuals without letting them know that you are there for that sole purpose. Do you have any questions?"

Hector read the translated letter and saw the names listed. The only one that stood out was that of Jack and Mary Marteau. Though he hated the woman with a special kind of passion, he knew this was a favor for Mark, and he felt honor bound to protect them as if they were his very own family. "Is there any intelligence on who the possible assassin might be?"

"As far as we have gathered it appears to be a couple living here in the United States. They're moles, but we don't know who they are, or their histories."

Hector remembered Mark mentioning that Nicole and Dylan were his friend Dave's family, but he wasn't about to volunteer that information to Joe. Mark described his relationship to Dave and Nicole as they drove toward Todo Santos, Baja California in 1987. They treated him like a brother, though Mark also dabbled in illegal drugs supplied to him by Dave. *If he chose to keep that a secret, then I will make sure, it would remain a secret.* "When do I start?"

"Be there on September 11. I would suggest you tail the Bakers. From what I have from the State of Washington's Department of Licensing, they have a 1981 Chevrolet Camaro, license number 627 VBN. And here's their current address."

He handed Hector the printout from the Department of Licensing that gave the details of Nicole Baker and her son Dylan, who just recently became a licensed driver too. There was also a short rap sheet of her arrests and convictions of minor possession of marijuana and driving while impaired. Obviously, her life since her husband's murder has left her very vulnerable. "Can I count on you to do this, without Mark's knowledge?"

Hector nodded briefly, still more focused on the minor misdemeanor arrests of Nicole Baker.

"Agent Gonzales, I need a verbal affirmation on this."

Hector snapped out of his train of thought and immediately replied, "Yes sir."

September 11, 2000

Hector arrived at the address in a mobile home park at a small town called West Richland. Mark told him his dad had moved them there initially in 1968, then found a bigger house on Thayer Street two years later. He described to Hector how backwards the town appeared compared to where they lived in Wenatchee, Washington. "There were no sidewalks and few if any street lights to help illuminate the darkness," Mark told Hector on that 1987 mission. His biggest complaint, Hector recalled Mark saying, "Were the wind and dust storms that blew in seemingly all the time, leaving me wanting to go back where I came."

According to Mark, he met Dave at Chief Joseph Junior High School and became instant friends. "Drugs weren't even in the equation then," Mark said. "Nicole was my neighbor before we moved in '70. I introduced Dave to her and they became sweethearts in high school."

He described this part of Mark and Dave's past to Hector as they traveled to Todos Santos. He remembered the good times before Dave got involved in the drugs and Carlos Lopez. At the time, Hector never gave Mark's story much thought. But now, as he looked over the darkened doublewide mobile home, all those descriptions of Dave and Nicole came back to him.

The more details he remembered from that long-ago conversation, the more he felt comfortable about trying to protect the small family that had been through so much already. Then there was the assassination itself. What damage has that done to this family? Obviously, they never moved from this place to escape the ghost of Dave. *It appears that their dark past will try to rear its ugly head again*, Hector thought.

He saw the white Camaro pull into the driveway at 6:45 AM. Hector saw Dylan, the teenaged son, pull himself from the driver's seat while Nicole slowly made her way out from the passenger seat, looking exhausted and old, though Hector knew her to be around the same age as Mark.

Hector drove to Mark's parents' house on Thayer, a wide two-lane avenue with sidewalks and tall beech, birch and cottonwoods lining the street. Long ago, when Richland was a government town, a virtual alphabet soup of homes was built. "A" houses were single-family dwellings for managers and higher, "B" houses were duplexes shared by foremen and supervisors and "C" houses were prefabricated homes of one or two bedrooms for the many workers there. Mark's parents lived in to a remodeled "B" house where they converted the duplex to a single-family dwelling. Now that Mark and his sisters had moved out and gone on with their lives, the house appeared too much for them.

Hector never forgave Mary for her disrespectful attitude towards him when he went up to visit Mark back in 1990. He parked the Crown Victoria fleet car he assigned himself at a nearby ballfield, far enough away that they wouldn't feel intimidated by his presence and they could continue to live their lives in relative privacy, but close enough that should he see anything suspicious, he could nip it at the bud, so to speak.

"I will gladly save Jack, but his mother, I would do it reluctantly," Hector said to himself aloud as he saw Jack doing some autumnal gardening with some flowerbeds in the front yard. Twenty minutes later, a neighbor woman came by wearing a light jacket over shorts, met Mary as she did some light leg stretching in front of their home. Mary wore Terrycloth-like material sweatpants and sweatshirt with white tennis shoes.

Hector saw both women begin a slow and steady walk down the street. He noticed how much they had aged in just ten years. Jack's hair appeared completely gray, as he slowly moved about the flowerbeds and Mary's fire red hair had turned a dull orange tint as she walked with a knee brace and a cane. *She must have had knee surgery recently.*

The morning of September 11 appeared to warm as the dew from the night before evaporated. All the lawns appeared manicured, green and lush as he noticed many of the people who lived there were senior citizens of mid to late sixties, seventies and older. *These people should watch out for each other. I bet they lived together in this neighborhood for thirty years, or better. I'm sure if they saw something, they would call the police.*

He called Joe to give him an update. *I will need to do research on this Serbian Security Service. I never heard of them myself, though I am sure every country has an internal agency charged with espionage and protecting its security.* "Joe, yeah I'm at the Marteau house. He is gardening, and she just went for a walk with a neighbor lady. Is there any more information on the possible assassins?"

"Nothing has come up yet, though NSA did see a package sent from Belgrade, destined to an address in Chicago. I have agents there checking it out," Joe replied from Spokane.

"How much longer do you want me here? I mean, if these assassins are not even in this state yet, what is the point? I could be doing work on digging these people up and who or what they represent," Hector stated to his boss.

"Hector, I want you to continue watching the Marteaus until about noon. Then you can rest. I agree it appears like a waste of time. I already informed local police of your presence at both locations, in case they get calls from concerned citizens," Joe Armstrong stated. "Do you have any questions?"

"If they're moles, how long do you think they lived here?"

"I have no idea," Joe answered honestly. "They could have recently been planted. I couldn't imagine government assassins being here years and years before being given an assignment."

"I'll talk back with you later," Hector stated before disconnecting the call. To his chagrin, he noticed Mary and her friend coming up on him from his back, when he glanced at his rearview mirror, they slowly and steadily walked down the sidewalk. "Please God, don't let her see me if she looks inside the car." Both women walked passed him, seemingly oblivious to him as they chatted about some local concern that Hector knew nothing about.

After noon, he went to his assigned hotel at Hampton Inn. He wished he brought his golf clubs when he saw a golf course nearby. He went to his laptop computer—he logged in to the bureau's assigned computer. Using a government search engine, like Google, tried to gauge whom these people could be. Hector began his research.

However, try as he might, he could not find the right keyword that would allow him to get the results he needed. After three hours, he had to walk away, getting nothing but a headache for his efforts. He laid down on the bed and fell right to sleep, not awaking until darkness of night descended on his room.

October 16, 2000

Hector could not believe his eyes as he saw a black Crown Victoria pull across from Nicole and Dylan's home. He covertly pulled up his night-vison scope to catch a glimpse at who this person was. *A Hispanic looking man,* Hector said to himself. He could not be certain if the man even noticed him from where he parked, up the street next to an empty lot. *Is he the assassin?*

Hector watched him, seeing what his next move would be. However, all this man did, was sit and watch the still empty house until just after sunrise when Dylan drove his mother home and they went inside. Hector saw him pull out a cell phone and could lip-read the man mouth in Spanish,

"They're here." A moment later, he drove away, still seemingly oblivious to Hector's presence.

Hector slowly pulled from the vacant lot and, keeping a constant, but visual distance, followed the man in the black Ford sedan. The car travelled upon the By-pass highway and merged onto I-182 and headed into Pasco, where he pulled off at the US 395 exit and then Hector could just see him pull in at the Motel 6. Hector continued driving north to the King's Truck stop and called Joe Armstrong. "It looks like I got company."

"What do you mean?" Joe asked as Hector could hear the lack of sleep in his voice. *Do I sound like that too?*

"A black Crown Vic, apparently the same style as the one I have, parked at the Baker residence until they showed up from work. He called someone. He's Spanish speaking, so it's possible he works for Che Lopez, but I don't think he's the assassin."

"Where is he now?"

"He's at a Motel 6 outside Pasco. I followed him there," Hector replied.

"I'll double check to make sure he's not one of ours from another department, or even CIA."

Why would the CIA be snooping around?

"I don't believe they are," Joe stated as if reading Hector's mind. "But, at the same time, nothing these people do surprises me. I did get some information on the two possible assassins, though it is extremely vague. It appears the two assassins go by pseudonyms of Clockmaker and Red Widow, and that is all we have. There are no photos and no description of who they are or what they look like." After a moment Joe asked, "Where were you at in relation to the car?"

"I was about fifty meters away near an empty lot. I saw him mouth out 'on yegado,' which means…"

"They arrived," Joe cut in remembering his high school Spanish. "But, how…"

"I can read lips, especially when the person is talking in Spanish," He replied.

"How do you know?" Joe asked.

"I was using a scope."

"Well, you're full of surprises," Joe said with a sound of amazement in his voice.

"After a bit, I'm going back to that motel to check out the car and get an idea of who owns it."

"I'll see if I can get more information on this 'Clockmaker and Red Widow.'"

"I can't believe there is no intelligence on those two," Hector stated with frustration in his voice.

"That's the nature of our intelligence gathering; everybody is paranoid and very protective of their secrets. It's something that will backfire on us with devastating consequences."

After an hour, Hector drove back to Motel 6 and saw the Texas license plate on the back of the black Ford sedan. Hector thought it odd that this car would be out of Texas. *That is Salazar cartel territory*, Hector thought. *I could see California, Arizona or Western New Mexico, but not Texas.*

He wrote down the VIN number and contacted National Insurance Crime Bureau and to confirm his suspicions; someone stole the car four months ago near Santa Fe.

He called Joe back, "Yeah, the vehicle is stolen."

"I'll get hold of Pasco Police and we'll get that guy out of our hair. Hopefully he's here illegally and will be sent back to Mexico where he came from."

"Thanks," Hector replied. "Is there anything more on Clockmaker and Red Widow?"

"Very little; obviously they came into this country under assumed names, but we can't seem to find them. It's as if they're invisible," Joe added in frustration.

Mark awoke Hector out of a dead sleep, as his cell phone buzzed on the nightstand next to his ear. He lifted the phone and saw it was Mark's cell and he reluctantly answered with a groggy "Yeah."

"You son of a bitch, it sure is great to hear from you bro. I got some great news to share with you."

Hector heard background noise and a Spanish voice of a young lady ask him for a drink.

"What? Yeah, get me one more. It's crazy over here, Anyway I got that case solved. A nun helped me frame a fairy-ass dressed up like Mother

Superior and got him to confess to those murders. I got that faggot sonofabitch tagged and bagged!"

Hector could smell the booze over the phone as Mark rambled about his latest accomplishment.

"Hey, I got to go and I'll see you later. Bye amigo!"

He heard the phone go dead as he muttered, "You drunk sonofabitch," and fell back to sleep.

Hector called him the next day to congratulate him while watching Mark's parents' house. "Yeah, that was definitely one for the weird case files," Mark told Hector. "Are you still on assignment?"

"Yeah, though the information that we've received so far hasn't panned out to anything worthwhile," Hector replied, being purposefully vague.

"So, you're at a dead end?"

"It appears that way," Hector, replied hopeful Mark would leave it at that.

"Well, I got a lot of work still to do to help the DA here to get this case to trial," Mark stated.

"Remember Mark, Puerto Rico has the same type legal system as Mexico. Your job is done; it's up to the defense to prove that he didn't do what you're charging him for, and if he confessed, then the trial is all but over before it began,"

November 27, 2000

Hector saw a minivan drive past his position near the Baker residence. It parked there, and the driver appeared to be doing something, and then he left. That is odd. Hector wrote it down in his notepad he had inside his heavy coat. He pulled his night-vision scope up and looked at the tall, clean-shaven man writing on a pad. Hector then focused his attention to the license plates in front of him; Illinois plates with the numerals, no letters that read 87 9887.

He could hear the cold winds of November buffeting the car door. Hector wanted mild winters of Southern California, not this cold crap that made him long for his home country.

For the next two weeks, he saw the same van appear at the same time with the same clean-shaven driver, writing in a notepad and then, after ten minutes, he would leave. Hector wrote all this information in his own little black notebook and relayed everything to Joe later after he finished his surveillance.

Hector observed a young mother with a pair of red-headed girls walking by the Marteau residence. She glanced at the house briefly and walked on down the street. Mark had called him, mostly out of boredom. He helped the San Juan Police and the district attorney to tie any loose ends to the case they worked on tied into a pretty bow for delivery to the court. "Remember Mark, your job is pretty much done now. So, stop worrying about it. You got the guy's confession, right?"

"Well, Hector, thanks for the legal advice on Canon Law. The DA already briefed me on its many nuances including burden of proof being on the defense's side. Anyway, I must get back to work here. Have a good one."

"You too, amigo," Hector said as he disconnected the call. I do not remember seeing her before.

December 13, 2000

Hector awoke with a start and bolted upright in his hotel room bed, as he felt cold sweat on his brow and he witnessed three coffins lowered into the ground. He saw the digital alarm clock read 2:40 and he forced himself up with an effort. *After working this case for three months, absolutely nothing has materialized. I am convinced this is a complete waste of my time and the Bureau's money.* He got dressed and reheated the pot of coffee in the microwave. Hector never cared for the taste of fresh brewed coffee, preferring day-old coffee instead.

As he drank from a white to go-mug, he continued to think how this had become a fool's errand because, except for a couple of blips on his personal radar screen, nothing has come of this investigation and Hector felt disillusioned, lonely and tired.

An hour later, he arrived at the Baker residence, until they showed up from work. He noticed that Toyota van didn't make its normal round at the usual time, which should have set off an alarm in his head, but perhaps because he felt so fed up with this case, it never occurred to him. He then went to the Marteau home. He could not understand why he felt this foreboding apprehension. *It is almost as if whatever happens, I will have no control over its outcome. It is as if I would not be able to stop what is about to happen.*

As he drove past the Marteau house, he saw them both inside the living room, as the table lamps cast a yellowish glow from the opened curtains. He noticed were in a conversation discussing whatever married couples discussed at 7:30 in the morning. He parked near the park, as he always had these last three months and he opened the latest intelligence fax from Joe.

In it, were a pair of grainy black and white photos along with the information on the Illinois license plate he gave Joe. It was registered to a Kolar, first name Danvar. However, according to Immigration, no such person existed here. In addition, according to authorities in Bosnia, relatives identified a body matching that name in 1996. Hector looked at the two photos that were extremely hard to see in the early morning light of a gray and overcast morning.

Hector caught a glimpse of Jack Marteau walking quickly from his house and getting into his Chrysler 300M and leaving. He immediately called Joe to find out what just happened.

"Yeah, Jack Marteau just left suddenly."

"There is a report of a fire at a storage unit in West Richland. From what I've gathered, he keeps a Recreational vehicle—one of those Class B or C motor homes at that storage area."

"That can't be coincidental," Hector stated as he noticed that same young mother with her twin daughters going up to the Marteau house. "Now, some lady has come over to the Marteau house with two young girls."

"What does she look like?"

"She's kind of tall and slender with red hair. I'm assuming those two girls are her daughters. Mrs. Marteau just let them in; so, I guess she knows her."

"Are you getting the idea this might have been someone's idea of a hoax?" Joe asked Hector with more than a hint of frustration in his voice.

"Outside of whatever happened at that storage lot just now, I would tend to agree. It does feel that way."

"Yeah, I think you're right. I'll call the local police and fire investigator to see what they think. Keep doing what you're doing I guess."

"Okay, she and the kids are leaving with what appears to be baking flour in a large plastic baggy."

"Alright, keep me posted and I'll let you know about the fire."

"I called Mark the other day to congratulate him for solving that case in San Juan," Hector said with a hint of envy in his voice.

"I know you would have been happier down there, but this is just as important. Plus, I had hoped this case would have been resolved months ago," Joe replied.

"He said it was one for the weird-case file."

"Yeah, I read his investigative reports and it reminds me of those Green River killings over in Seattle back in the eighties. He had high praises for the nun. I guess she and a pupil of hers cracked the case and Mark caught a pedophile priest who had just been appointed bishop there."

"I'll talk with you later," Hector said before disconnecting the call. *That should have been me down there helping to crack that case.*

December 14, 2000

Hector heard his cell phone ring about seven, just before the Bakers arrived from their shift at Denny's Restaurant. "Yeah, what's up?"

"I want you to go to an apartment complex about two blocks from the Marteau residence. It is off Marian on Williams. Local police believe a minivan fitting the description off video surveillance, was seen parked at the storage unit just prior to that motor home fire."

So, it is suspicious, Hector declared to himself. "I'm on it," Hector stated, glad to be doing something worthwhile for a change. He drove to the apartment complex that to Hector looked old and neglected. He saw the minivan parked in front of an apartment, with the Illinois license plates. *This just might be the break I need.* He cautiously approached the van and looked inside, and then he went to the apartment's door and knocked but heard no commotion inside to indicate anyone was home.

He heard a voice behind him; an elderly sounding female voice that asked, "Can I help you find someone young man?"

"Yes, I'm looking for the owner of that van parked there. I'm Hector Gonzales of the FBI," Hector replied quickly fishing out his identification and badge to show her.

"I see; well Helen Merkel rents the apartment and if there is no answer, then she must be gone, taking her oldest child to school. I could tell her you stopped by, Mr. Gonzales."

Hector thought a moment and realized he did not want to scare her off if indeed she was the Red Widow. "No, that's quite alright. I'll come back another time; it's not that important; Thank you for your time, ma'am."

He went back to his car and thought about waiting for her to show, except for the fact that a little voice inside his head kept nagging at him that something just did not seem right. Hector abruptly left the apartment and headed directly to the Marteau house. He noticed, as he passed the brightly lit living room—appearing the same as always—that maybe he had over reacted a bit. He noticed the young mother and her twin daughters walking down Thayer on the opposite sidewalk. One little girl waved at him with a wide, welcoming smile and Hector waved back.

He parked at his usual spot and sat there for the better part of an hour, when he realized that no one had come out from the house yet. *The cold, overcast morning may have something to do with it,* Hector thought. *Normally, Mary is outside trying to stretch her groin and hamstring muscles to go on her usual walk, or Jack is outside doing chores to keep him busy,* Hector told himself. His fears became realized though when her neighbor friend showed up and knocked on the door and received no answer.

He immediately got out from the car and ran towards the woman, giving her a start, until he pulled out his billfold with identification and badge. "I'm with the FBI," he called out to her. He attempted the door, but it felt secured when he jiggled the door's handle. Then he ran to the back where the door leading to the kitchen stood and he heard the neighbor woman follow behind at a discreet distance.

Then, he saw the bodies. Jack sat in a chair at the kitchen table, his eyes glazed over, a look of disbelief etched upon his face, while Mary lay sprawled on the tiled floor, still dressed in her housecoat and slippers. Hector heard the woman gasp.

"Oh, dear Lord, are they dead?"

Hector could only nod as his heart sank and he realized he had failed his friend. He went to dial 911.

"This is 911. What is your emergency?" The middle-aged sounding dispatch operator asked in a crisp, professional tone.

"I'm Agent Hector Gonzales of the FBI; I'm reporting a possible homicide at 4711 Thayer Street."

"Are there any weapons involved, Agent Gonzales?"

"Not that I'm aware of," he replied when a light went off inside his head. The mother and the two girls! It felt like an awakening, as the grainy black and white photo of the Serbian girl and the mother of the two-young red headed girls were the same person. *I must go back to that apartment.* "Look ma'am, I got to go. The police and coroner are on their way, correct?"

"I have a police officer heading to that address right now, if he isn't already there," she replied.

Hector searched around to see if any police cruisers had arrived while he had been on the phone with the dispatch operator. In the distance though, he heard the obvious sound of a wailing siren steadily approaching. "Okay, I hear a siren. Here's the thing, I think I know who done this, and time is of the utmost importance…"

"Sir, I can't make the car come any faster than it already has…"

"That's okay, the car has just arrived, bye."

The officer saw Hector, who he immediately profiled as the primary suspect, as he got out from his cruiser with blue and red flashing lights illuminating the slate gray December morning pulling out his Glock .40 and demanded, "Get on the ground, now!"

"Yes sir," Hector said as he immediately complied with the officer's order. "I have my identification in my inside left front pocket. I am also carrying a Glock .40 on a holster on my right hip."

"You got a permit, Pedro?"

"Really, officer? I'm a special agent of the FBI, and my name ain't Pedro, it's Hector, Hector Gonzales," he replied while the officer frisked him and found the hand gun, along with his identification where Hector said it would be.

"What are you doing here?" He asked Hector with suspicion in his voice as he read the pieces of identification and saw the gold Federal Bureau of Investigation badge attached to the billfold.

"I've been tasked to offer surveillance and protection of the Marteaus. Their son is also an FBI agent."

The officer listened to Hector's story as he called his supervisor. "Yeah, this is Officer Rogers. A man claiming to be an FBI agent is here. Name is Hector Gonzales. Seriously? Well okay. Can you get hold of his supervisor?" He nodded and then disconnected the call.

"You're to call your boss at your earliest convenience," the officer stated. "Sorry for me flying off the handle like that," he apologized as he handed Hector his gun and billfold back to him.

"You were doing your job, man. I totally understand your procedure. Now I got to go and see if that murderer is still around." Hector ran at a dead sprint to the Crown Victoria and took off down the street, engaging blue flashing lights just inside the front grille.

He arrived back at the apartment but saw the van gone from the parking space. Dread filled the pit of his stomach as he went to the apartment and knocked anyway; hoping someone might be inside, but no one answered the door. He then walked directly to the apartment manager's office, which was nothing more than an apartment itself, just with a desk in the living room and other office equipment in the dining area, including a PC with printer on a table. The same woman he talked to earlier sat at the desk looking over a ledger opened and spread out on the desk.

"Hello, I told Helen that you were looking for her. She thanked me and said she'll be right back and took off," the Landlady said breathlessly.

"Her name isn't Helen Merkel; it is Lena Costas aka the Red Widow. She's an assassin."

"Oh dear; are you sure?"

Hector nodded. "Can you let me inside?"

She at first appeared reluctant, then stood up from behind her desk and grabbed her coat, with a large ring of over a dozen keys and led Hector to the apartment. She quickly unlocked the door, as her mind felt jumbled by this sudden intrusion and all this tragic and circumstantial news that she had been fooled by a very beautiful family, who were not who they said they were.

She allowed Hector inside. The apartment had no furniture, no dishes, no cleaning tools or supplies. It appeared as empty as if no one had ever been there at all. "Son of a bitch," he exclaimed in frustration.

He pulled his cell phone out and contacted Joe Armstrong. "I found the Red Widow, and now she's gone, and Mark's parents are dead. This is probably the worst day of my life, Joe."

"I'm on my way down there, Hector." The call signal went dead as he disconnected the call.

Hector returned to the Marteau residence to see a dozen or so police cruisers, along with a pair of vans, one marked Coroner on its sides parked up and down the street. Hector slowly made his way to the house as he saw the police and county sheriff deputies securing the crime scene and conducting their initial investigation. CSI investigators began removing and categorizing everything in the kitchen. They were especially interested in a plate with a pair of half-eaten pastries. One of the investigators opined, "I would guess baklava." He took a small sample and placed it on his tongue. "It has a bitter almond flavor; it's apparently cyanide."

"We wouldn't get a confirmation on this, until six to eight weeks when the bodies will darken," another CSI investigator stated.

"We'll have to remove the contents from their stomachs and that will be the confirmation. Can I help you?" the investigator asked Hector as he watched them work.

"Hector Gonzales, FBI. I was tasked to protect this couple; their son is in the FBI too."

"I'm sorry for your shitty luck. Although you are an agent on an official capacity, you still cannot be here while we conduct our field assessment. Any contamination of the scene could potentially destroy the case against whoever did this."

"I understand," Hector said. He left the CSI specialists to perform their jobs as he looked at Jack's back yard. *In spring, summer and early fall, he had a lush lawn with five different fruit trees, and a vegetable garden towards the back where a six-foot tall cedar fence bordered his property. The yard smelled musty from the remaining leaves decomposing on the barren ground; it smelled of late autumn now*, he surmised.

He suddenly remembered that smell in the apartment. It was a strange odor, as if it was masking an even more offensive smell. *However, what odor would they be hiding?* He caught the officer who initially treated him as if he was a suspect and said to him, "I have a hunch about something. Can you come with me, Officer Rogers? I want to check something out."

"I can try," he replied as he got on his portable Motorola and called his sergeant. "Fourteen, you got a copy?"

"Fourteen here, announce your traffic."

"The FBI agent, Gonzales wants me to go help him investigate something at another location, over."

"Where at?"

"Tell him, it's at the apartment where the suspects were staying," Hector said to the officer."

"Fourteen, it's at the apartment the alleged suspects lived at," the officer responded.

"Affirmative; inform me if you find something," the sergeant said.

"Will comply, over."

"Roger, out."

"Okay, Agent Gonzales, let's go and see if we can find something, "Officer Rogers told Hector as he put away the portable radio and started walking smartly to his patrol car.

Hector went with the officer to his cruiser, its overhead red and blue lights still revolving inside a long clear plastic cylinder as mid-day approached. They drove back to the apartment. Hector went inside the apartments' office and retrieved the landlady.

"What is it now, Agent?" She asked in frustration.

"Look, I'm sorry if I'm screwing up your day, but I need back inside that apartment."

"Again? This is twice now. I don't have time for this, young man."

"Please, there is something about the smell inside that apartment that didn't seem right," Hector persisted.

In a huff, she pulled herself out from her office chair, grabbed the keyring and walked passed him toward the apartment. Hector followed.

The officer could plainly hear the elderly woman complain bitterly at Hector, "I don't understand what you're getting at young man. It smells perfectly fine in here. It's a pleasant smell, like lavender and something else? I can't seem to place it, a potpourri aroma, perhaps?"

"Exactly," Hector exclaimed. "It's masking something else in there that might be more unpleasant, and perhaps more incriminating…"

"Like gasoline?" the officer quipped, as he began searching each room, sniffing the air to try to discover that other odor.

"You got it man. I have a feeling that the person, who caused that fire, also left something here. Hopefully, anything they left might possibly save another person's life," Hector continued as he too sniffed in places the officer had not gotten to yet.

"I found something," the officer called out.

Hector ran to the back bedroom where Officer Rogers held a single rag, but Hector realized right away that it possessed the slight but certain odor of gasoline. "You got an evidence bag?"

"All that stuff is in my car. I'll place it back on the floor and go get the evidence kit," he said and left the room.

"Oh dear, and they seemed like such a nice family too," the landlady said with such sadness in her voice, Hector suppressed his emotions with a cough. "She said that they came here from Germany in hopes of a better life. Now it seems I've been fooled by them."

Hector did not say anything to her, though he wanted to so bad, it hurt. The officer brought in an attaché case and opened it up to reveal an assortment of evidence gathering tools including zip-lock baggies that Hector placed the gasoline-soaked rag inside and sealed it. He pulled out a marking pen and wrote down the time and date on a white strip embedded on the front of the bag. "You got a magnifying glass in there too?"

"Of course," the officer replied as he grabbed a magnifying glass and handed it to Hector.

Hector began meticulously probing in between the carpet fibers to see if he could find anything else, wires or insulation that could further prove the Clockmaker was also here. *I doubt the Red Widow set the RV on fire; that wasn't her MO.* After over an hour, he found nothing else. "Damn, I was sure hoping I could get more here."

"There's always the dumpster," the landlady volunteered.

"Of course!" Hector shouted with glee. He and the officer ran out to the dumpster and saw two things that could incriminate their suspects: a partially empty cake pan of baklava and a pair of wire cutters. The officer got inside and grabbed both and placed one in a standard sized zip-lock bag, while the cake, Hector just had him get a sample of the cake to throw into the baggy. "Let's dust for prints, Officer Rogers."

After the officer pulled himself out from the dumpster, he used talcum powder that he liberally poured onto the baking pans and shook the remaining powder back inside the container, and then checked for incriminating fingerprints. All they both found though, were children's sized fingers that Hector concluded were the two little girls'. *She and her husband must have used latex gloves throughout,* Hector thought.

Both men went back inside and continued dusting for more prints, but still they could only find the fingers of small children all about the apartment, confirming Hector's suspicion.

Satisfied with their find, both went back to the cruiser and the officer reported to his supervisor, what they discovered.

"Good job," the sergeant said to both and then said, "Agent Gonzales, if you ever get tired of the grind of being a federal agent, I could sure use a good detective like yourself."

"Thanks for the offer, but I think I'll be happy doing what I'm doing for a while," Hector replied.

When they arrived back to the Marteau residence, Joe Armstrong waited for Hector to return.

"We need to talk," Joe told him as soon as they got out from the car.

"Okay, we can talk here in front of God and everybody, or we can wait until tonight when we're at my hotel room," Hector responded with such determination it set Joe back a step and the officer found himself an excuse to go somewhere else.

"Very well, we'll wait until tonight, but I shouldn't have to tell you how totally fucked up this is right now."

"I agree with you one hundred percent, sir."

The talk began at Hector's hotel room and ended in a lounge by the golf course, though the course itself was closed for the season, a few die-hard golfers kept the bar open in the off-season. Hector felt as if he was betraying his friend, yet he understood where Joe was coming from on this too. *Mark would want blood for his parents' murders, and nothing else would do. He compromised on his friend Dave's assassins; not really since the actual shooters themselves died at my and Mark's hand, but the man who ordered the hit, Santiago Lopez-Sanchez, is in prison only because he had a bounty and Mark needed him alive.*

"I have a friend in the coroner's office who owes me a favor. He's going to rule the deaths naturally caused, and the murder investigation, along with the evidence, is going bye-bye."

Hector stared down at his half-finished tequila shot and wondered if Mark would do the same thing if he were in his shoes. "Are we still going to protect the Bakers?"

"Of course," Joe replied with surprise in his voice. "I'm working on getting them into a witness protection program; something I should have done from the outset but thought you and I could nip this before this thing happened. It's the worst possible scenario I could imagine."

Hector could only nod in agreement, as he continued to stare at his drink. "I suddenly feel tired, Joe. I'm ready to go back to my room."

"I understand," Joe replied with a touch of empathy in his voice to sound concerned for his subordinate. "Trust me, this is for the best and we can't ever tell Mark the truth about what happened today."

"Yeah, sure," Hector replied with his body hunched over and his face drawn and looking old and tired.

December 15, 2000

Hector never really slept that night, and what sleep he did have wound its way around that promise he made. Joe can't live forever. When Mark finds out, all hell will break loose, and yes, I will probably be hated for a while. One day I will tell him what happened to his parents, and how sorry I am for his loss.

He totally forgot about the Baker house surveillance, so when he awoke with the sunrise at
7:30, he cursed himself for his failure. He immediately dressed and drove out to the Baker house
and saw all was well, as Dylan and his mother had
come home without incident and were most likely
just now going to bed after working all night. It felt
so odd to him now that he did not have to watch
the Marteau place anymore. He drove by there
where crime scene tape was strung along the four-
foot cyclone fence in the front yard, and the police
secured the front door with a special seal, initialed
by the coroner, which could not be removed without a judge's order.

He went to the Denny's Restaurant on George
Washington Way and ordered a south-western
omelet. Hector drank dark coffee and read the
local paper. Not surprisingly, no mention was made
concerning a homicide at the Marteau residence.
Hector thought, *I'm sure the coroner already contacted
Mark's sisters about the loss, or maybe it was Sheriff
Dickerson? Regardless, now would be the wrong time
to shoot the bull with Mark; he would be beside himself
with grief by now.*

His cell phone rang, and he answered, "Agent
Gonzales, how may I help you?"

"It's Joe; meet me at the Richland Police station off Jadwin on Swift. You know the place?"

"Yes, I'll be right there." Hector disconnected
the call about the same time his omelet arrived. Not
being one to let good food go to waste, he helped

himself to half its contents, then asked the nineteen-year-old blonde waitress for a to go-box, and then went to the police station.

"Here's the thing, Agent Armstrong, this is a homicide investigation and until I get something from President Clinton himself telling me this isn't a homicide, I ain't backing off," Sheriff Tracy Dickerson told Joe. Dickerson wore his evergreen uniform with four stars on the shoulder tabs, as the two-stood toe to toe to each other.

When Hector walked into the Richland Chief of Police office, he also noticed the perfectly bald Chief of Police wearing his blue uniform and four stars on his collar, the CSI investigator, who had a bemused look upon his cherub face and the coroner who looked completely pissed off. Neither participant noticed Hector when he entered. They all seemed more focused on the fight that appeared inevitable.

He walked over to the Captain of Crime Scene Investigations and asked, "What did I miss," in a hushed tone.

"The sheriff got word the FBI tried to quash the investigation, citing national security concerns and the sheriff called bullshit on that."

"Shit, sir, for once would you tell the truth," Hector yelled out in frustration.

"You stay out of this and that's an order, Gonzales."

"No, you Gonzales tell me what this is really about," the sixty-seven-year-old sheriff ordered Hector.

Joe Armstrong gave Hector a cold, hard stare, daring him to blurt out the truth.

"Sir, the truth is someone put a hit out on Mark's parents, and on the Baker family. The two assassins I believe are still in the area, though they left the residence where they were staying these past two months," Hector replied looking directly at the sheriff.

"Then why in hell are we keeping a lid on this?"

"The hit originated out of Todos Santos Mexico," Hector replied. "NSA intercepted a letter from Che Lopez to a Serbian leader of the Serbian Security Service to put out a hit on the parents and friends of Mark Marteau."

"You are in big trouble mister," Joe said under a controlled rage.

"No, I think you are the person who's in trouble," Dickerson replied as his own anger boiled over. "Mark is my friend and I have known him since 1977. Even if Che pulled the trigger himself, there's no way Mark would be any less of a man by doing vigilante justice."

"I don't want to take the chance," Joe responded heatedly.

Then, an explosion erupted that shook everyone and everything in the room. "What the hell was that?" Hector wondered.

Then radio chatter erupted stating a car exploded in front of the post office near the Federal Building. Everyone left the office and got in their vehicles going two blocks south to the Federal building. It didn't take Hector long to see the white Chevrolet Camaro, fully engulfed in flames, was none other than Nicole Baker's. There appeared to be one bystander, apparently hit by flying glass and the blast's percussion, which killed him instantly. Hector could see it wasn't Dylan, but an older man, who never expected this day to be his last.

An hour later, after they pulled the blackened body from the smoldering wreckage, the CSI captain stated to Sheriff Dickerson, "She's obviously female from her breasts; early to mid-forties would be my guess." Hector had no doubt, who she was.

Joe came up to Hector, his face pale, as if he was physically ill by all he witnessed. "We have to be in this together, Hector. Please, please promise me you will not tell Mark about this. Like I told you before, I don't want a rogue agent on my team going vendetta on me."

"Is that all you're worried about? How this would look on you? Yeah, I will promise, sir. Now with all due respect, get the fuck out of my face," Hector yelled at his superior with a white-hot rage that he had not felt against another human his entire life. He looked at Nicole's sheet covered body, along with the anonymous person under the other sheet as the CSI team rapidly worked on her, gathering any evidence in this fresh case.

But, where is Dylan?

Just as Hector asked that question, with his back to the street, a Toyota minivan with a family of five drove by the scene. The older little girl took a picture of the destroyed car and the white sheeted bodies lying on the ground from her camera phone.

October 15, 2014

If Che had not known about Dylan until it was too late, would he had done something about it? It's possible he might not have ended up a prisoner in his own home. We'll find out when we get there, I suppose. I should have revealed my secret four months ago after Joe Armstrong's funeral. Hell, I should have told him on the way down here from out in Bum-fuck nowhere but didn't. Mark needs to know. I will have to tell him soon.

"Hey Mark, I need to tell you something."

"So, tell me, Hector," Mark replied while yawning and fighting off sleep; drove to the airport's entrance.

"Better yet, it can wait. I'll tell you when we're done."

END